D0915720

an explanation
for chaos

The Body Is Water (novel)

An Explanation For Chaos (stories)

an explanation for chaos

julie schumacher

Published in the United States of America by
Soho Press Inc.
853 Broadway
New York, NY 10003

Library of Congress Cataloging-in-Publication Data

Schumacher, Julie, 1958–
p.   cm.
Contents: Reunion—The private life of Robert Schu-
mann—Levitation—Dummies—Infertility—Dividing
Madelyn—Rehoboth Beach—An explanation for chaos—
Telling Uncle R.
ISBN 1-56947-070-7 (alk. paper)
I. Title.
PS3569.C5548E97   1997
813'.54—dc21   96-47316
CIP

Manufactured in the United States

10   9   8   7   6   5   4   3   2   1

credits

Grateful acknowledgment is made to the following publications in which these stories first appeared:

"Reunion"
California Quarterly
The Best American Short Stories 1983

"The Private Life of Robert Schumann"
Atlantic Monthly
Prize Stories 1990: The O. Henry Awards

"Levitation"
Minnesota Monthly

"Dummies"
Atlantic Monthly
Prize Stories 1996: The O. Henry Awards

"Dividing Madelyn"
New Letters

"An Explanation for Chaos"
The Quarterly

"Telling Uncle R"
Sonora Review

For my parents, Frederick and Winifred, the original storytellers; and for my sisters, Joan, Anne, Kathryn and Barbara, listeners all.

table of contents

reunion

It wasn't till years after the operation that I realized my mother would never have died from it. She came from a long line of unscrupulously healthy women who had dedicated their entire lives to surpassing each other in maturity. They no longer counted their age in years, but in reunions, and nothing under fifty was counted at all.

My mother lived for the reunions. Every year and a half she would dress us up and lead us, trembling and fearful, to the skirts of our grandmothers, great-grandmothers and great-aunts. They towered over us at an impressive height, their legs thickly swathed in flesh-colored stockings. My sister and I were left to ourselves during the ceremonies; we looked wistfully on while the women were photographed, smiling and blowing out huge numbers of birthday candles, more set against the idea of death every day. Their pictures still hang on our living room wall, so close together a finger can't fit between the frames.

* * * * * * * *

It was the first time that any woman in the family had gone into a hospital. My cousins wouldn't even go there to give birth for fear people would suspect them of going for something else. Naturally my mother was questioned, cajoled and warned against the dangers of lost reputation, but she went anyway, taking the largest of the reunion photographs in her suitcase. It was a newspaper clipping of her great-grandmother's sisters seated around a silver trophy bearing the slogan of the American Longevity Association. Their names were listed in order of age in the caption.

* * * * * * * *

My mother left on a Thursday. The only thing she said before she shut the door was, "Take care of your father." She always worried about him.

"What for?" said my sister. She and I were the only ones home with him and didn't know how to take care of a fifty-five-year-old man. We didn't want her to go away; at a distance she would seem more vulnerable. Anything that happened to her would be our fault, anything we did wrong was bound to cause her pain.

My father took it harder than any of us. He hadn't really expected her to go, and just the day before he'd made her angry by pointing out that "hospitalization" would go down on her work record. He wasn't trying to hurt her; he only wanted to know where the pain was.

"Is it something to do with your . . . being female?" he asked, spotting me in the doorway.

She told him it wasn't, that it was something much less serious than he could imagine, and that certainly didn't deserve to be on a permanent record.

"Why should I have to imagine? Why don't you tell me so I don't have to imagine?"

"I'm much stronger than you might think." She was already making arrangements to take her Christmas vacation in August.

"What will I do while you're gone? What will the kids do? What will they think?" His voice warbled.

"They know there's nothing wrong with their mother." She smiled at me and I thought of all the times I'd stepped on the sidewalk cracks and then gone back to erase them, rubbing the soles of my shoes sideways along the pavement. "And I've already provided for your food."

When she wouldn't tell him the name of the hospital he accused her of making it all up.

"Why are you bothering with all this?" he asked her.

She was silent so he turned to me.

"Your mother isn't like anyone else," he said.

. . . .

When we told him she'd gone he called all the hospitals until he tracked her down at Northern Memorial, but the operator said my mother's number was unlisted.

"What room is she in?" he asked.

"I'm not allowed to give out that information," said the operator.

"Well how big is your hospital?"

"Thirty-six floors."

My father was dumbfounded. "Do you know what she's in for?" he asked.

The operator said she didn't know.

. . . .

My mother called the next day, but wouldn't give us her room or phone number. She said she was fine. She didn't want any visitors, and told us not to send flowers, the room was full of them from the families of other patients. (The flowers we'd already sent were later returned in a cellophane bag, a note taped to the outside with the message: "Put these in the dining room—big yellow vase $3/4$ full of sugar water.") She asked about my father and we told her he was angry about the unlisted number and didn't want to talk. She sighed and told us to watch that he didn't get upset.

My father was furious.

"She didn't even *ask* to talk to me?"

"No, she just asked how you were. She told us to watch out for you."

He didn't want to know anything more about it. He had the extension wired for the next time she called so that he could hear without being heard, and he would answer all her questions while laughing to himself that she didn't know he was listening.

. . . .

Once in a while the woman who shared my mother's room would call for her, explaining that my mother was busy—getting signatures on a petition for fresh vegetables on the lunch trays. We didn't know what to say to the woman, but felt obligated to talk to her since my mother had asked her to call.

"What are you in for?" we asked her.

"I'm a kidney patient," she said.

"Kidneys?" said my father, shouting into the dead mouthpiece.

"Your mother's a very nice person. She talks to everyone," said the woman.

"What does she say?"

"She talks about sports and politics, you know."

"Well tell her we said hello."

"Tell her we don't want to talk to any more kidney patients," said my father.

When my mother called back she wanted to know how my father was doing. "Does he ask about me very often?" she said.

I looked at my father's back in the hallway. He was sitting on the floor with the extension to his ear, his legs spread straight in front of him. He looked like a bear in a picture I'd seen once.

"All the time," I said, and I saw him shift the extension to his other ear.

* * * * * * * *

One day I found him staring at the space left on the wall where my mother had taken the picture.

"Something's missing," he told me.

"She took it with her," I said.

"There are no men on this wall," said my father, ignoring me.

I looked. There were no men on the wall. The men in my mother's family weren't important; no one knew anything about them except who they were married to, and as soon as they'd produced a few children they seemed to disappear. On the other hand it was well known that my maternal grandmother had once set fire to her own home rather than see it knocked down, and at the height of the blaze, jumped out a second-story window to the ground, her eighty-three-year-old legs sturdy as a cat's when she landed. My great-grandmother came to America on a freight ship, disguised as a sailor, and before reaching shore had been promoted to first mate.

"I guess the women live to be older," I said.

"It looks like a family of clones," he said. "Not a man in the group. There's no pictures of your mother, either."

I looked. Everyone in the pictures was at least sixty-five. "She's probably not old enough," I said.

He searched the house until he found a picture of my mother, and then he put it on the coffee table. It showed her gardening, leaning over the tomato bushes in the back yard, perspiration stains up and down the back of her shirt. It was a good likeness. She seemed about to stand up, and the way she bent over the tomatoes made her look even stronger than usual. She could have been an advertisement for vegetables. Photographs always had a way of immortalizing her; even when she was standing next to me I'd imagine her in a different pose. I had a collection of them in my head, and she was different in every one.

* * * * * * * *

My great-grandmothers brought us casseroles and desserts, dropping them off on the step after dark so the neighbors wouldn't see them and start asking questions. They must have been communicating with my mother in spite of their disapproval; one dish of manicotti came over with a tiny envelope on its lid, and the note inside said: "I never use ricotta cheese, it's too expensive. Cottage cheese is just as good and I'm sure they won't know the difference. M." We passed it once around the table and let the dog lick the dishes. My father got angry because we didn't leave enough on our plates.

"Jesus Christ, what's the dog supposed to live on?" he shouted.

It was obvious the strain was affecting him. He still refused to talk to my mother on the phone, but he started giving us lists of questions to ask her: whether the doctors were men or women and how old they were, how many people shared her room, how many times a day she got to eat . . . Sometimes he would sit with the receiver to his ear for hours after she'd hung up, and whenever I walked by him in the hallway he would block my path with his legs and ask me another question.

* * * * * * * *

The next time my mother called she said we shouldn't expect her to call so often, that she wouldn't be calling for two or three days. She said she'd be having an operation, a small one, but that everything was fine, there was no reason to worry.

My father almost tore the extension from the wall. He started shouting into the receiver saying she'd promised it wasn't serious, saying she had to come home immediately. She could hear his voice from the echoes bouncing into the kitchen, and she shouted back, "I'm fine, Frederick, they're just going to fix me up a little." When the echoes subsided she said, "Tell your father I'll be fine."

He didn't believe it. He told us all the horror stories he'd ever heard about hospitals.

"During the war there was a man," he said, "a Polish general, who was so weak he couldn't eat. By the end of a month he was shrunken beyond recognition. They'd starved him almost to death, and it was up to his wife to get him out of the country. She had to wrap him in blankets and pull him across the border in a toy wagon."

"You mean she disguised him as a baby and nobody could tell he was really an old man?" we asked.

"He wasn't supposed to look like a baby," said my father. "How could a sixty-year-old man look like a baby? You're missing the whole point."

"Well what does it have to do with Mommy's operation anyway?"

He shook his head as if we were being stupid.

* * * * * * * *

The day of the operation I found him hanging a picture in the empty space on the wall. It was a photograph of an old man wearing a brown coat and a bland expression.

"Who's that?" said my sister.

"My Uncle Jack. He lived to be eighty-seven."

"That doesn't sound very old," we said.

"Just by comparison. No one in your mother's family ever dies. People in my family die early."

"What do they die of?" we asked.

"That's beside the point." He walked to the opposite wall, took a picture of my mother out of his wallet, and tucked its edges into the corner of a reunion photograph, smoothing it down with his thumb. "Way beside the point." It was a newspaper clipping of my mother on the median strip of a highway, a white flag tied to the antenna of her broken-down VW. The picture was taken by a helicopter during the worst traffic jam of the year, and my mother was looking up and waving just when the camera clicked. She was just big enough so that I could recognize her.

"What does all this have to do with Mommy's operation anyway?"

"You don't like the picture?" said my father.

"That's not the point," I said.

"No, I guess it isn't," he agreed.

. . . .

She came home on a Saturday. The front yard was covered with blackbirds fighting over crusts of pizza we'd thrown out the night before, and as my mother walked over the grass she shooed them away, picking up the crusts and bringing them in the house. "What have you been eating all this time?" she asked, waving the mutilated crusts in front of her. My father took her by the hand and sat her down on the couch. She had a long red scar across the front of her neck.

He was speechless. This had never happened before; it was the first scar in the family, the end of an era.

"Did it hurt?" he asked, finally.

She got up and walked over to the mirror. The scar went straight across the front of her throat, but wasn't obvious unless she tipped her head back. She tilted her head carefully, still looking in the mirror, and ran her fingers over the bluish-red skin, pulling lightly down with one finger and up with another.

"Does it hurt now?" asked my father.

"No." She turned and saw the picture of Uncle Jack on the wall. "Who's this?"

"No one," said my father.

"Why is he hanging on the wall then?"

"He's the one they dressed up as a baby," my sister told her.

"He was *not* dressed up as a baby," shouted my father. "That was *not* the reason for the toy wagon."

He turned to my mother, who had just discovered her own picture. She took it down and put it between the encyclopedias.

"Are you sure it doesn't hurt?" he asked again.

* * * * * * * *

We worried about her from then on. She slept a lot. My father rented a mechanical bed for the living room and we took turns raising and lowering her legs. We never pushed the button that moved her neck even when she said it didn't hurt.

When she started talking about the next reunion, and said she wanted to be in the picture, my two great-grandmothers came over to talk her out of it. They saw the mechanical bed and looked politely away.

"You're not even gray yet," they said. They saw the picture of Uncle Jack and squinted.

"I want to be in the picture," said my mother.

"Aunt Gladys thought you were dead and buried."

"I want to be in the picture," she repeated.

They sighed. "Do you have something with a high neck?"

My mother nodded.

* * * * * * * * *

Two months later it was on the living room wall. Uncle Jack had been taken down, and in his place stood my mother, dressed in a blue turtleneck. The scar was completely hidden. Since she was off to one side it was hard to tell whether she was meant to be in the picture or if she'd just walked in by accident. But she looked beautiful, and my sister and I imagined her in blue for a long time.

Aunt Gladys had come up after the candles were blown out. "I thought you were dead and buried," she said, clutching my mother's arm. "What a relief."

Eventually the scar lost its color and settled into a fold in my mother's skin. She said the doctors told her not to drive; the bones in the back of her neck will always be weak.

* * * * * * * *

It wasn't till years afterward that I realized my mother would never have died from it. At night she still stands by my bed in the dark, telling me not to worry. Whenever she leaves the house, or pulls the car out of the garage, I tell myself, my mother is stronger than anyone else's.

I see her driving down the highway, she waves to me and my heart swells. I see her crashing into the car just in front, her whole neck giving away, her head faltering, my mother, the car crossing over the median and bursting into . . . No. It was only a small accident, she's all right, it didn't hurt for a minute. There's my mother standing on the median, safely out of the wreck, thumbing a ride. I know she won't slip, the trucks going by won't even come near her, and soon, someone will roll down their window and offer to take her home. She waves once more and the helicopter pulls back, snaps another picture, another, farther and farther away until she's just a normal woman on a highway, no one's mother, no scar on her neck at all. Cars speed past in both directions, here she is by my bed, her hands cool on my back in the dark. We can sleep peacefully, knowing my mother is immortal. There she is on the highway, there in the yard, leaning over tomato bushes in the garden, and I can bring her back whenever I need her.

the private life of
robert schumann

Before Mr. Zinn came to teach us music, we were bored every Wednesday and Friday afternoon. We'd had to study with a woman named Miss Fox, who scratched herself with a pointer, and who died of a heart attack one day in the coatroom, clutching the sleeves of a dozen jackets in her arms. With Miss Fox we'd had to learn "This Land Is Your Land" and the national anthem on two different instruments: we had a choice of the autoharp, the recorder, the triangle, and a pair of blocks. The blocks had sandpaper stapled to their sides. If you couldn't play you had to sing, so most of us banged and strummed away, while Miss Fox counted time at the front of the room, her worn heart pounding like a tired drum.

We had one week free of music after she died, and then the district hired Mr. Zinn. He was only the third male teacher in the middle school, and he didn't look like Mr.

Hickman, who taught phys. ed., or like Mr. Vandeveer, who wore a suit and had a white goatee. Mr. Zinn was young: he had short, wavy black hair and sideburns, and watery eyes that protruded farther than they should. They were round like the eyes of a lizard or a frog.

The first day back we noticed instantly that the autoharps were gone. The recorders and triangles and blocks were missing too; the music table held only a record player and an enormous pile of books.

"Sit," Mr. Zinn said. You'd think he was talking to a dog, but we heard nothing cruel in his voice, so we sat down. On the board we saw his name, Francis J. Zinn, and the date, March 3. "How many of you know anything about music?" No one raised a hand. "That's what I expected," he said. "That's why you aren't going to play. There's no use trying to play an instrument if you don't know anything about music's *source*, its fountainhead. Who's been to Europe?"

Few of us had left Delaware, except for occasional trips to the Jersey shore.

"To understand music," Mr. Zinn said, raising himself on tip-toe and slowly lowering himself back down, "you need to understand Vienna, Leipzig, Schiller. Who knows what I mean by *strophic* and *durchkomponiert*?"

No one spoke, and Mr. Zinn began to fill the board with words. We learned that Vienna crossed the Danube like a bridge, that Beethoven went deaf, and that almost everyone related to Johann Sebastian Bach had the same first name. By the end of the class we still hadn't said a thing. Mr. Zinn turned to Valerie Kenny. "Tell me something about music that you'd like to know."

Of the twenty-one kids in the class, probably twenty of us would have been stumped for what to say. I would have tried for something correct, because that's what I do. But Valerie was strange.

"I'd like to know if you knew Miss Fox."

"We were acquaintances," Mr. Zinn said.

"Were you sad when she died?" Valerie was pale and thin and feverish, and we made fun of her for the veins that shone through her skin. We didn't yet understand that she was pretty: she had long tangled hair the color of almonds, a reddish mouth, and fingertips that glowed.

"That's an unusual question." Mr. Zinn folded his arms across his chest in a gesture that seemed borrowed from a book. "I suppose I'd have to say that I was. Yes, I was sad. Any other questions?"

Lois and Chuckie and I were laughing at the back of the room. "I'd like to know if Valerie's retarded," Lois said.

Mr. Zinn blushed. We'd never seen a grown man blush, the color rising up his neck like juice in a glass, and blooming when it reached the level of his ears. "Thank you," he said. Clearly, he'd never taught school before.

* * * * * * * *

I knew Mr. Zinn already, because he directed our choir at church. Not because he was Methodist, my mother explained, but because he earned money from the service every week. Whenever I dropped a dime in the collection tray, I imagined it going straight to Mr. Zinn.

Our church, as vast as a cavern, was left from the time when the city wasn't a slum, when it held white doctors and their families instead of the poor. Now the church was seldom filled, but it was still white, the stubborn doctors and their wives driving in from the suburbs to spend an hour beneath the massive gold-leaf dome and think of

God. They could *believe* more easily in the presence of matching marble fonts and leaded glass, a hundred pipes for the organ, an immaculate burgundy carpet, and wooden doors that two men together had to push to admit the sun. The back of the church held a balcony, the front a gigantic stained-glass window showing Jesus, hands tipped out as if he'd heard of crucifixion, surrounded by children twice my size, and enormous lambs.

I was in the confirmation class that spring. We had to study the parable of the good Samaritan and sing in front of the congregation in a special program at the end of the year. Methodists—the ones I knew—loved to sing. They tapped their feet impatiently through the sermon, browsed the hymnal during prayers, and sang *Amen* in twelve-part harmony as if God himself directed from the floor. My lack of enthusiasm for hymns was a family trial. My mother would push the hymnal toward me, point to the verse (we sang them all), and sing in a voice as high and perfect as a dream. I had a scratchy alto voice that sometimes buzzed. It was always lost between octaves and I used it sparingly, whispering along with the choir on refrains.

Every Sunday for half an hour the confirmation class practiced two shorts hymns: "O for a Thousand Tongues" and something about sheep that we sang as "mutton" just for fun. Mr. Zinn directed us with an atheist's determination. We hummed with our mouths half open, snoring the words, while he blinked and pressed his lips together, as if struggling to overcome with his own effort our lack of it. On especially bad days he'd set down his baton, run a hand through his wavy hair, and approach the line. "Keep singing," he'd say, and we'd try another verse while he drew near, his red tie flapping over his shoulder. He'd start in the second row and walk past each of us, head bent low as if in prayer, to find out who was singing out of tune. Sometimes he'd pause at a single mouth for quite a while, coming so close to our lips with his well-scrubbed ear that we couldn't sing above a whisper, afraid of damaging the parts that lay within. We didn't know where to look when he hovered close: breathe, and his inner ear was moist; sniff, and the hair at his sideburns brushed your nose. I dreamed of shrinking to the size of a crumb and climbing in, exploring the hammer, anvil, stirrup, and shell: it was pink and barren there, and my voice, when I let it go, spun cascading through the arcs and tunnels, sweet and clear.

* * * * * * * *

The autoharps and the recorders never reappeared. By the second week we were building instruments of our own. He called it "Musicshop": we made banjos from oatmeal boxes and rubber bands, whistles from pens, drums from aluminum cans and Playtex gloves. While we worked, Mr. Zinn played records and told us stories about the music we listened to.

"Schumann was a true romantic," he explained. "He liked to read Byron. He was Schubert's successor as the master of the German *Lied*."

"That's World War Two," Chuckie said. He was building a flute. He took it home every few nights and got his father to fix it up with a welding torch.

I was working with Lois, who had asked me to be her partner because she wasn't capable of doing anything alone. "Forget it," I said, when I looked up from my plans and saw her bushy yellow hair, the constellation of freckles on her skin.

"What do you mean, forget it? You and me are building a trumpet. Just like this." She showed me a wrinkled magazine picture of a black man playing an instrument with at least a hundred metal parts.

I looked at the picture of the trumpet and then at Lois. "What do we make it from?" I asked. I'd finally decided to build a xylophone with sticks.

"I've got these." She showed me a plastic bag full of cardboard toilet rolls and mismatched copper wire. "Once we're done we can paint it gold."

I didn't ask her how she expected it to sound. Lois got mad fairly easily, and I didn't want her yelling at me in class. That's how our friendship worked: when she wanted something from me, I always said yes; when I wanted something back, Lois said she wasn't sure. I admired her for her confidence and style.

. . . .

Mr. Zinn liked to sing during class. He paced the room with his hands carving gestures in the air: *"Nun hast du mir den ersten Schmertz getan. . . ."* He had a beautiful tenor voice; when he took a breath and spread his hands, tilting back his head so the veins in his neck stood out like string, we knew he imagined himself in another place and time, dressed in leotards and a blouse on a moonlit stage.

He rarely looked at our projects. He spent most of his time filling the board with scales and notes we couldn't read, or brooding by the window at the back of the room. He smelled of chalk dust and shampoo, and we learned to pinpoint his location by his odor as he paced between the coatroom and the window. We craved his recognition and his words. When he did stop to check the progress of our work, throwing his tie over his shoulder as he squatted down, we had the impression he was studying our lives, that he held our souls, and not a cigar box or a hammer, in his hands. He didn't treat us the way the other teachers did; I wondered if he realized we were young, or if he even understood what children were.

"The world is full of mediocrity," he said, sometimes to himself and sometimes to us. "Nothing is worse. Failing is better than being simply good at what you do." He picked up Chuckie's flute. "Failure's a virtue, next to undistinguished skill."

"Practice makes perfect," Chuckie said.

"No, unfortunately, it doesn't. Practice breeds *competence*, not perfection." Mr. Zinn examined the flute, by far the best-looking instrument in class. "Look at Schubert. He wrote symphonies, some of his best, at the age of eighteen. He suffered depressions all his life, but in a single year he wrote almost a hundred and fifty songs. He died of typhoid at thirty-one, a physical wreck. He was utterly ruined."

"It's just a saying," Chuckie said.

"Perfection comes from genius, or from God." Mr. Zinn turned to me. "Doesn't it, Jane?" It was the first time he'd singled me out. I had glue on the tips of my fingers, shreds of cardboard in my teeth. I wanted desperately to say something clever and uplifting, something that would cause him to bring up my name in the teachers' lounge.

"Yeah, I guess," I said, smiling so that he would know I understood my limitations, that if I was dumb it was through no fault of my own.

Mr. Zinn put the flute on the desk. "What are you smiling at?" he asked.

"Great move," Lois said, when he walked away.

. . . .

We noticed the ring on Valerie's hand at the end of March. Lois and I sat together in science class, with our desks pushed close so that she could cheat, and when she kicked me, I looked up and saw Valerie rubbing the stone on her dress to make it shine. It was a dark green gem in a wad of gold, with a square insignia on either side. It was much too big for her finger; it slid up and down over her knuckle, as bright as chrome.

"Where'd you get it?" Lois asked, poking Valerie in the neck with a felt-tip pen.

"Don't, you'll stain me." Valerie lifted her hair and revealed the ink. Her neck was petite, a perfect stem. The ring was visible through the woods of her tangled hair.

"That's just a school ring," Chuckie said. "Everybody buys one when they graduate, that's all."

"Where'd you get it?" Lois asked again. She wasn't whispering anymore, and Mrs. Hardimer, the teacher, gave us a look.

"It's probably her dad's," Chuckie said.

We tried to pretend we didn't care, but Lois couldn't let a problem go unsolved. During gym we trapped Valerie in the bathroom and asked again. She was using the middle stall, so we stood on the toilet seats on either side and leaned over the top. "Tell us whose," Lois said.

Valerie let the top of her gym suit fall, and we saw her chest, as smooth and flat and white as ours. She didn't cover herself with her arms as we would have done.

"We're going to start spitting when I count to two."
Lois draped an arm across the door to block escape.

Valerie flashed the ring. The stone was as green as a
parrot's eye. "Okay," she said, "it's Mr. Zinn's. He gave it
to me Friday afternoon."

"He didn't *give* it to you," Lois said.

Valerie shrugged and pulled up her gym suit, showing
the name tag with her name embroidered upside down.

"He probably just let you see it. Friday you'll have to
give it back."

"I don't think so." Valerie sat down on the toilet, fully
dressed. When we looked down at her from above, she
seemed tiny and pure.

"Look how small," I said to Lois. But Lois was running
through the double doors, racing with the other kids
outside.

. . . .

He didn't ask for it back on Friday, even though Valerie
wore it around her neck on a silver chain.

"We aren't positive it's his," I said to Lois after school.
We were riding bikes in the parking lot between the
teachers' cars.

"Are you saying Valerie's a liar?"

I came around the side of a VW bus; we were face to
face. "Maybe not on purpose. I mean, not like you or me."
I looked at the gap between Lois's teeth, big enough for a
coin. "Maybe she wishes it was his. Maybe she has a crush
on Mr. Zinn."

"That's disgusting." Lois made a narrow passage by a
Plymouth, scraping the yellow paint with her handlebar.

"Careful," I said, and she kicked a dent in one of the hubcaps with her shoe.

"We have two more years of this place, and I think it stinks. I'm going to be a rifle girl in high school." She put her kickstand down and twirled an imaginary rifle, taking aim.

"You don't get to shoot," I said. "Those rifles probably aren't real."

"Nothing's real." She pulled the trigger. "Not even you." We rode the long way home through the empty lots, bruising our tires on tree roots and jagged stones. A block from our neighborhood Lois stopped. "Here's where Valerie lives," she said. "I came here on Halloween last year." She pointed to a house that wasn't like any of the rest. It didn't have shutters or a sidewalk or a porch or a basketball court. It looked like a pile of wooden boxes stacked on top of each other so that some of them jutted out. The yard was overgrown with raspberry bushes and weeds.

Lois wanted to spy on Valerie through the first-floor windows, so we parked our bikes and crept through the neighbors' yard to station ourselves in the brush at the side of the house. As soon as we took our positions, Valerie's mother, Mrs. Kenny, appeared with a folding chair and a sunhat and a camera, turning the lens on us where we stood.

"I thought I'd get a look at who was breaking into the house," she said, focusing on our hands on the window-sill. Seeing Mrs. Kenny was always scary: she dressed like us, in pants and T-shirts, with her hair in a ponytail or a braid, while all the other mothers dressed in skirts. At one of the parents' days at school she showed up with a paint-brush in her jeans and her hair full of dirt. She was disconcerting—she made us feel as if we might just get larger instead of older when we grew up.

"We were looking for Valerie," Lois said.

"Oh, I see." Mrs. Kenny nodded. "Did you try the door?"

"We thought it was stuck."

"Try it again," Mrs. Kenny said. "I'll watch from here. You can turn the handle and go right in."

We traipsed to the door like zombies.

"Second left," Mrs. Kenny called, and we went inside.

Valerie sat on the bed in her room, holding a wooden box between her knees. "I've told my mom not to do that," she said. "She hijacks kids my age and sends them in."

"Your mom is cracked," Lois said. She looked at the box.

"No, but she thinks I ought to have visitors," Valerie said. She lifted the lid and we saw the folded squares of paper, as tempting as cream. "Do you want to know what I have in here?"

"It doesn't matter," Lois said. "We don't really care."

"I'm not supposed to show you." Valerie chose a note from the top, easing it open fold by fold. "Do you want to see?" We craned our necks as she smoothed the paper against her thigh. "This one's the first."

It was a drawing in black. It showed a flute with a person's face where the mouthpiece was. The eyes were closed, and around the head was a mass of hair.

"Where'd you get it?" Lois asked.

"Here's the next." Valerie unfolded another square. The second was a drawing of a harp, like the prow of a ship, but again with a face and hair. It was drawn very lightly, the eyes of the harp half closed and the mouth half open in a smile. She showed us a violin, a guitar, a drum, and several instruments we'd never seen. All had the same dreamy eyes and tangled hair, and not a word appeared on any page.

"Mr. Zinn gave you these," I said. I recognized the paper from his desk.

Valerie looked pleased, and some of the pallor disappeared from her face and arms. "That's what I thought." She folded the notes and stashed the box in her underwear drawer. I saw the ring still dangling from its chain around her neck. "I'm taking lessons. I'm learning to play the piano after school."

"This is stupid," Lois said. "You don't know they're from him."

Valerie smiled, showing her gums. "At first I found them in my desk. But the last one I found in my jacket pocket, so he must have put it there during lunch."

"Still, you don't *know*," Lois said. "You aren't sure."

"He's going to teach me about the composers. Private things. He says I remind him of Clara Schumann."

"You don't even brush your hair," Lois said.

"He called me Clara once," Valerie said, not even listening anymore. When we left, she thanked us for coming. "It makes my mother happy," she explained.

. . . .

That night at dinner I wanted to talk. I had something to say.

"*What,*" my mother said. She finally put down her knife and fork. "What's so important that you have to interrupt?"

I felt the weight of what I knew on the back of my tongue. I had all of it there: Valerie was getting notes from the teacher, we never played music in music class, and on Sundays Mr. Zinn was a different man. I had all of the knowledge ready, and felt certain that if I phrased it right it would be of interest to anyone. But when my mother and father turned to me, I forgot which part came first; I couldn't remember how it all made sense, the way I'd figured it out before.

"I'm not going to eat these carrots," I said. "They stink." My parents ignored me and went on talking, as if I were someone else's child or had never been born.

* * * * * * * *

Lois ignored me too. Something was lost: she refused to answer the phone at her parents' house, and at school she sat by herself at a broken desk. When I tore our trumpet into shreds, letting the cardboard glide and settle in the trash, she didn't care.

Though she wouldn't talk to me anymore, she sent two notes. The first was from the library encyclopedia. I knew it was from Lois because of the smudgy fingerprints and the fact that the page was torn out of the book. Under the heading "Robert Schumann" was a blurb about Clara Wieck: the name was underlined in blue. It said that Clara was Schumann's wife, that she was the daughter of Schumann's teacher, and that Schumann had met her when he was eighteen and she was nine. The difference in ages, it said, didn't matter to the two, who finally married, despite objections, when Clara turned twenty-one.

The second note Lois wrote herself. "Everything makes me sick. That includes you." I found it in my jacket pocket after school.

I blamed Mr. Zinn for everything that went wrong. Now

when I sang in his ear in church, I thought of Catholics, the way they whispered through a wall to a waiting priest. I thought about humming softly in his hair, so softly that he'd put his ear against my mouth. I thought of whispering in that pink and marbled maze, *I've seen the notes. You told her not to show us but she did.* But I sang "O for a Thousand Tongues" and waited for the opportunity to speak.

Chuckie said it wasn't possible—no one Valerie's age had a boyfriend half that old. "He must be thirty or forty," Chuckie said. "You guys are nuts. Is that what you've been fighting about all this time?"

We were riding bikes at the top of the block; Lois was trying to jab a stick through the spokes of our wheels. "You wait," she said. "Just wait one minute or two."

"I've got to go in and take a bath," Chuckie said, but he didn't go. Lois had called both of us on the phone and told us to meet at the top of the hill, at the dead end over the highway that we weren't allowed to cross. It was seven o'clock, and the shadows of our bikes had thinned and gone. We circled a few more times, listening to a pair of beagles down the block, and then Lois braked. We saw Valerie and Mr. Zinn in a light blue Ford on the highway. The car slowed down on the opposite shoulder, and from the embankment we saw only their arms and legs beneath the roof: Mr. Zinn was wearing a sweatshirt, not a tie, but Chuckie recognized his watch. We saw him reach across Valerie's lap and open the door. When she got out, he pulled away, without waiting to see where she'd go.

"Hey," Chuckie yelled, and Valerie looked up. The air was thick with mosquitoes and lightning bugs, and we seemed to be looking at Valerie through a screen. She made a dash across two lanes to the yellow line and stood between streams of traffic, shifting from one foot to the other, small and pale. When she finally crossed the other lanes and reached the bank, pulling on reeds as she clambered up, each of us extended a hand to help her climb.

Valerie continued on her own. Her knee socks were balled around her ankles and her sweater was buttoned wrong. She reached the top and brushed herself off and immediately started down the street.

"Were you at school all that time?" Chuckie asked. We began circling on our bikes.

"I had my music lesson." She walked with tiny shuffling steps to avoid our tires.

"Your lesson's on Tuesday," Lois said. "From four to five." We expected Valerie to cry. We needed her to: her tears would tell us who was right and who was not, they would reconfirm our places in the world.

"He isn't a boyfriend," I said, "or a friend. If it was me, I'd make him drive me to the door."

"It wouldn't *be* you," Valerie said, not angrily but as if stating a simple fact. We stood in the darkness of the trees for a little while.

"Mr. Zinn's married, you know," Lois said. "Jane sees him every Sunday in the choir."

In fact I hadn't said he was married; I only said he was old enough.

"She's seen them kiss," Chuckie said, making a smooching noise with his lips against his arm.

"That isn't true," Valerie said.

All three of them turned to me. I was the tallest and heaviest; I felt the stature of my flesh, the heft and decisiveness of my organs, busy at their work beneath the bones.

"She can prove it," Lois said. And I said I would.

* * * * * * * *

My parents were surprised I'd invited friends to confirmation, but I told them we were supposed to bring guests, so they didn't care. We picked Valerie up—she was wearing a sun-colored dress and a bright straw hat—and drove to Lois's, down the street. Lois sat on the stoop wearing a pair of jeans and roller skates instead of shoes. "I can't go," she said. "I have to help my mother clean the house."

"How are you going to help if you're wearing roller skates?" I said. I leaned out the window and threatened to pull out her teeth with pliers if she wouldn't come.

Lois turned and skated down the walk, making an *rrrrrr-clack-clack* sound as she rolled away.

My parents dropped us off in front of the huge oak doors of the church. Walking in was a vision: you took a program from the usher and entered the floodlit stained-glass air of the center aisle. Valerie started for the doors, but I pulled her back.

"You can't go in that way if you're not a member."

She looked surprised. "I thought anyone could come."

"You can visit, but you have to use the entrance over here." I led her into the basement, down a narrow, dusty hall away from the church, to the choir's practice rooms and the vestry, where the sound of handbells and the scent of heavy robes dulled the click of our footsteps on the tiles. We walked up a flight of stairs to the treasurer's office, past the custodians and the gift shop on the left. Valerie pulled my arm. "The altar's down there."

I shook her off. She could barely follow me up the narrower steps to the tower; I let myself run, I let my clumsy legs unfold and carry me through the DO NOT ENTER door and down the dead-end passage above the sanctuary. Valerie had dirt on her dress; she was breathing hard. She nearly tripped around the final corner, slamming into me where I'd stopped at the secret place. Above our heads the massive stained-glass window bulged like the side of a balloon. It was five or six times our height, pressing outward toward the wall. The first time I saw it, I was shocked: the colored panes were lit not by sunlight but by a hundred ordinary bulbs. But most disturbing, the people in the window *faced* you. I had expected to see the backs of their heads, but their eyes, in brilliant topaz and aqua blue, met your gaze on either side.

I peered through a broken pane at the window's edge. The pews were filling up; the ushers collected their silver plates, and the organist cracked her knuckles on the rail. Mr. Zinn stood off in the corner, wearing a robe, not white like the minister's but black, with enormous flowing sleeves. His wingtips gleamed in the yellow light from the chandeliers.

Valerie still gazed above her head. The organ hummed a processional, sending vibrations through our shoes.

"Tell me," I said. "At your lesson. What do you do with Mr. Zinn?" It was time for me to line up with the rest of the class.

"He pulls the shades," Valerie said.

"But what do you do?"

The glare of the lights made the hallway warm. "Different things."

"Show me what they are."

Valerie squinted when she looked my way. I must have been haloed by the bulbs on every side. She reached up around my neck with her blue-veined arms and unbuttoned my dress. "Sometimes like this." She laid her palm, warm and sweaty, on my chest. The convocation began below.

"What else?" I said, and Valerie showed me where he touched. She was hiccuping, sending nervous bubbly echoes down the hall.

"You can't tell anyone," she whispered, her pointed chin against my chest.

Through the crack in the window I saw my class lining up in a pew.

"It's partly your fault, now that you've done it." She was warm against me, glowing like a coal. "You'll never tell."

I buttoned up as best I could.

Valerie helped me straighten my collar. "He isn't married, you know," she said, and I felt the tears welling up in my eyes. "I knew he wasn't all along." Her yellow dress held pieces of color from the window, and in its light she seemed to be broken into shards.

I turned the corner at a run, plugging my fingers in my ears so that I wouldn't hear.

* * * * * * * *

I walked up to the altar disheveled, out of breath, from a direction opposite that of everyone else in the class. Mr. Zinn blinked his limpid, startled eyes when I took my place; the other kids nudged one another and whispered until he lifted his baton.

Through the whole first song I didn't sing. I knew that the world was constructed solely for humiliation, that nothing was fair, and that being right would never matter in the end. I still felt the press of Valerie's hands on my neck and chest.

Between the hymns we were supposed to count to ten.
On eight Mr. Zinn looked up. He was listening, hand sus-
pended in the air, baton tip pointing straight to God. We
had our mouths half open, ready to sing, but the baton
stayed fixed. Mr. Zinn tilted his head to the side. In the
quiet that followed, we heard a noise barely audible,
coming from just above our heads, or from the vents, or
the organ pipes, or from the dome. It was a small, des-
perate sound, barely a whisper, but clear and distinct:
Don't tell.

Mr. Zinn could have kept right on, but he was a man
attuned to sound, and the voice that repeated *Don't tell*
had a certain music, like a chant or a primal song. The
organist took off her glasses; the minister scratched his
head, revealing a bold striped shirt beneath his robe.
People in the farthest aisles began to stir.

I thought I knew how the moment would end. I would
be denied, they'd pass the cup above my head, the wafer
would burn a hole through the flesh of my tongue. Valerie
would be rescued, starved and tear-stained in her dress,
and I would be left in the church alone, with the treasurer
loading coins into blue felt bags and the janitor pushing
his oblong broom between the rows. Mr. Zinn was pale.
He was combing the window with his eyes, searching for
Valerie, looking through the holy faces for her own.

I knew I had seconds before he found her, before
the three of us were called on to explain the things
we'd done.

I took a breath and began to sing.

levitation

Beanie Gandolfo showed up at the doghouse with a message for the dead. We should have refused and sent him home. He was only six, about the height of the dog-house roof, and there was a look of recent bereavement in his eyes. But Theresa and I were hungry for the fee; business was slow and we were saving for a Ouija board downtown. I told Beanie to sit by the doorway in the grass, and I took his dime.

It was the summer of '73, a year of locusts and toma-toes. Bright rotten fruit lay warm and trampled on the ground, and from the trees we plucked cicada shells to string with thread and needles. Theresa wore a strand around her neck. She smelled of licorice and dirt.

"The medium will be with you right away," I said, waiting for Theresa to take her seat inside the doghouse, facing out. Then I tacked the black silk curtain to the door so she could see through it but the customer could only see her profile, gray and dim. It was stuffy and dark inside with the curtain down, but never hot. We'd pulled the house to a shady spot at the back of the lawn where Theresa's German shepherd, Munger, couldn't go because he was tied up on a chain. He panted in the sun at the edge of the drive.

"Who do you want to contact?" Theresa's voice was echoey and low. Sometimes I wondered why she chose me, for the summer, as a friend. I felt lucky just to serve as her assistant, opening and shutting the silky curtain like a hinge.

Beanie squinted toward the veil. "You should know who I want to contact. You're the medium," he said.

He had a point. I started to think that what we were doing might be wrong. It wasn't an overwhelming thought, just a hint at the back of my mind, a fear that anything we touched could turn to stone. But Theresa was quick. At school the teachers always said she wasn't bright; they hadn't seen her with a client, one on one.

"We're in touch with a very large number of pets. If I have to read your mind, it'll cost you more."

We knew the dime was all he had. His mother gave him twenty cents a week. "Gloria," he said. "Her name was Gloria. She was orange, with a stripe. I had to bury her today."

"A goldfish?" We'd had dogs and guinea pigs and mice, but I had to admit that fish was something new.

Theresa started the chant, a sort of humming through the nose. "What is your message?" she asked, and Beanie wiped a hand across his eyes. Above us was a blue midwestern sky, an occasional cumulus drifting into view.

"I want to know what she's doing now. What she thinks of me," he said.

Theresa paused. It wasn't a message: it was a question, which we didn't allow. Usually she made the sender try again. But maybe she was tired of taking messages for pets; maybe a fish was just too small. Anyway, she stopped to think it through. I pictured Gloria in her bowl, her little stomach moving in and out as she filtered water through her gills.

Theresa knocked three times on the inner wall.

"Your response, Madam," I said.

Theresa hummed. "Gloria," she said, "is roasting in a firepit in hell."

. . . .

One of the first people to learn of that response was Theresa's dad. His name was Reverend Jacks and he was a minister, tall and Presbyterian, with wavy hair and wide, clean hands that he folded and unfolded when he talked. On the pulpit he looked like Jesus: there was a gentleness in his eye, but we knew he simmered underneath. When he talked he looked over our heads, as if he expected us to be taller than we were.

"You two are charlatans," he said. He demanded that we give the money back. What seemed to bother him most of all, though, was the meanness of the deed. "Where's your sympathy?" he asked, spreading his palms out to the light. I saw him whispering my name beneath the stars. "Didn't it occur to you that fooling him was cruel?"

It was a very good question; I had to answer yes and no. Yes, we did feel a slight uneasiness when Beanie got up and ran away, but no, we weren't sure it was cruel at the time, because judgments often aren't clear until after the fact.

Reverend Jacks ignored me. He put his hand on his

daughter's arm. "What about you?" In front of us on the grass was a pack of tarot cards we'd stolen from the five-and-ten downtown. "You have a bicycle," he said. "You have a dozen games inside. Can't you find something else to do?"

Theresa shoved her fists in her pockets, deep. We both wore silver rings on our smallest toes. "I want to levitate," she said.

Her father stared. He didn't seem to understand. "I won't have you acting unkindly. You will behave in a Christian manner to your friends." This was Reverend Jacks's real concern. But who was to say what was Christian? St. Ignatius floated on the air, and Jesus knew how to raise the dead. Was it wrong of us to aspire to even more?

I smiled up at Reverend Jacks, a beaming grin. He was by far the handsomest man I'd ever known.

He looked me square in the face and sighed. "You have to learn to walk the ground. How else can you expect to be adults?"

When he was gone, Theresa crawled inside the doghouse. "At least he didn't find these." She waved a pack of cigarettes that we kept on a shelf above the door. She looked like her mother. She had dark brown hair and a skinny face; her eyes were set close together, as if she'd been looking at something too long and then gotten confused.

I sat at the entrance on the grass, listening to Theresa replace our objects on the walls. We had a crucifix made of sticks, a thermometer on a string, a broken watch, and in a mayonnaise jar on a tuft of grass we kept Theresa's pet lizard, whose name was Lazarus and who didn't seem to mind the heat. Above the door we had a postcard of a man on a flying carpet with a turban on his head. He raised his hands as if in wonder at the stars.

The air inside was thick and gray and full of dog hair

that floated in the slats of light. The ceiling formed a narrow arch; it was studded with nails pounded in through the shingles above, so you had to be careful not to sit too close to the sides or rise up suddenly to leave. It was like a miniature cathedral: seated cross-legged in the dust, I couldn't tell if it was small or I was large. Breathing the heated air, I could imagine a place without color, where people floated noiselessly and drank their daily oxygen with straws. It was always a shock to emerge and see the grass and the wooden houses in a row.

"I've been thinking." Theresa poked me in the back with her foot, so I turned around. "We should have a séance. We'll have a séance Friday night."

"Your father won't like it."

"Who cares?" Her legs emerged from the doorway, skinny and tan. She pulled herself out. "Besides, he doesn't think any of this is my fault. He thinks you're a rotten influence on me."

"That's not very fair," I said. "I think you might even say that's unsamaritan."

"Judge not," Theresa said. "A loaf of bread into many fishes . . ." Her hands were folded in a church and steeple.

"Amen."

". . . will not the stone of sadness roll away from our hearts. We are a miserable . . ."

"Hallelujah," I said, crawling into the doghouse in her place.

". . . miserable bunch. Let's hear it for God. A walk across the water is worth two on a bush."

"Say it again." There was a smell of sweat and dust inside, and the light was pouring through a hole in the doghouse roof. "You know what'll happen, though, if we hold a séance Friday night."

"What?" Theresa dropped down onto the grass and we sat with our toes interlaced, me in the shade of the doghouse, she in the sun.

"We'll have to invite your sister, and your father will probably make us invite Morgan Rausch."

"Christ," Theresa said.

I'd sat with Morgan in homeroom. "She isn't that bad. She'll be harmless if she comes."

Theresa yawned and stretched her legs. "Morgan Rausch," she said, "is a lesbian from Mars."

Morgan's father was dead, and we were on orders to be nice. He died in the spring at the end of the school year, days that we spent staring out the windows at the fields of early corn in perfect rows. Morgan was absent for the last few weeks of class, but she came back for the final exam. She opened the door to Mr. Genly's room and stood there looking in. Morgan was always what my mother called "unusual" or "odd," but in the doorway she was clearly something more. She stood facing us by Mr. Genly's desk, and we saw that her hair—thick black hair she used to sit on, tucked beneath her in a braid—was now cut blunt above the ear; on her nose was a pair of glasses, as if grief diminished what she saw. But what surprised us most of all—and made Mr. Genly drop his roll book on the floor—were Morgan's clothes. She wore a man's button shirt, the sleeves rolled up half a dozen times to reach her wrists, and a pair of black creased pants cut off with scissors at the hem. A man's gold watch slid up and down her bony arm. Morgan looked like, and was, a 10-year-old girl in her dead father's clothes.

Mr. Genly got up from his desk and seated Morgan next to me. He handed her the problem set and watched her get to work. When I looked over at her paper, she was done.

Theresa passed me a note that demanded, *What did Organ write down for #5?*

Her father's dead, I scribbled back.

Theresa carefully folded the note and dropped her pink eraser on the floor. I picked it up. I read the tiny writing on the back. *That's not what I asked you,* it said in pen.

. . . .

Theresa got permission from her father to have a party Friday night. "He thinks it'll make me normal," she said. "He thinks we'll sit around discussing boys."

"Thou shalt not lie with beasts," I said, but Theresa waved her hand and closed her eyes. We sat together in the doghouse; I'd been reading from a copy of *Miracles of the Saints* that Theresa borrowed from the library downtown. I read aloud in the shafts of light; Theresa stopped me whenever I came to something good, and I'd have to read it twice or more. Her favorite part was on St. Theresa, which I must have read a dozen times.

"Read my namesake again," she asked, and eventually I didn't need to find the page.

"St. Theresa of Avila was seen lifted on the air as if with wings; and there she remained above the earth in contemplation many hours."

"It doesn't say how many hours?" I knew Theresa saw herself in robes, gliding out of sight above the trees.

"Nope," I said, peering through a knothole in the wall. Walking toward me I saw a pair of army combat pants, rolled up at least a dozen times below the knee. "Uh-oh. Visitor starboard side."

Theresa looked past me through the door. "Hey, it's Morgan. What do you want? What's the password?"

"I don't know any passwords," Morgan said. "But your mother's watching from the kitchen window."

I poked my head out the door and there was Mrs. Jacks, scowling from her place behind the sink.

We decided to emerge.

"Well?" Theresa looked at Morgan, then at me. Then she climbed on top of the doghouse, straddling its roof. Her heels just reached the edge on either side.

"Your mother said you wanted to see me," Morgan said. Behind the square black glasses she looked like a mosquito or a fly.

"What she means," Theresa said, "is that she thinks it would be nice if we wanted to see you. What we want is something else."

"What do you want, then?" Morgan asked.

It was one of those open-ended questions, like in school: there might not be a single answer, and the object could be just to make you think.

"Nothing," I said, but Theresa mumbled, "Plenty," and I realized she was right. But was there anything we wanted that we could have?

"I heard about the party Friday night," Morgan said. "Your mother asked if I would come."

"What did you say?" Theresa asked.

"I told her I would have to talk to you. Do you want me to come?"

Theresa frowned. "It doesn't matter very much. I guess I don't. I'd probably rather you stayed home."

"What about you?" Morgan lightly touched my hand.

It was an awkward situation. I didn't like disagreeing with Theresa, but it was hard to be rude at such close range. I knew that being an adult would be like that:

gradually learning to offend without embarrassment or fear. "I don't know," I said.

Theresa looked away.

"One against, one neutral." Morgan shrugged. "I suppose I'll have to reach my own decision. What time is the party?"

"Seven." I could see Theresa getting mad.

"Seven on Friday? Let me see." Morgan looked at her father's watch, which had a tiny gold calendar that snapped on the wristband, one for every month. "I'll flip a coin. Heads I go to the party, tails I don't."

"That's a weird way to decide what you want to do."

"This isn't deciding." Morgan took a dime from her father's pocket, which extended on the outside of the pantleg past her knee. "This is fate."

We watched the silver spin against the sky.

"Heads," Morgan said, uncovering the coin against her wrist and quickly putting it away. "Is there anything I should bring?"

Theresa turned her face up toward the sun. She didn't look down again until Morgan crossed the driveway, shut the fence, and disappeared.

. . . .

There were five of us Friday night: Theresa, her sister, Barbara, Robin McMann from down the street, and Morgan and me. Three or four others couldn't come, and Theresa was in a bad mood from the start. We spent the whole day pouring M&M's into bowls and arranging the furniture on the porch so we could unroll our sleeping bags. We must have moved the couch a hundred times.

"What's the matter with you?" I asked. "We're having a party. You got what you wanted after all."

Theresa looked at the decorations we'd picked out; the candles and the colored napkins shaped like oranges, lemons, pears. "I'm sick of this place. I'm sick of everything I see."

I reached for the M&M's but Theresa grabbed me by the arm. "And I'm sick of you and Morgan Rausch. You can sleep next to her, over here. I'll be sleeping by the door."

"Go ahead." I pulled my arm away.

"I might even sleep upstairs and leave the rest of you down here."

"Fat chance," I said. "Your father'll drag you downstairs by the heels."

"And you'd be the one to tell him. You know something, Frieda?"

"What?" I said, even though I knew better than to give her an opening like that.

"I'm only friends with you because there's no one else around. Back at school I'll start to pretend you don't exist."

"That doesn't surprise me," I said, but Theresa had already turned and left the room.

I went home for dinner and came back at seven o'clock. Theresa's sister, Barbara, who was nearly 14 and had clumps of hair beneath her arms, was sitting cross-legged on the couch.

"You're the first one here," she said, and I knew Theresa was getting lectured upstairs; I could hear her mother's voice through the vents above. "Never . . . matter of respect . . . civility," it said.

"This is bound to be a stupid party." Barbara was cleaning her toenails with a fork. "You know what I mean?"

We sat and listened to Mrs. Jacks. She was saying *Theresa Marie* in a voice we could have heard a mile away.

"In the entire history of the world," Barbara said, "you won't see a single party that'll be stupider than this."

Robin arrived. She threw me a look across the porch that plainly said, *What's the oaf doing here?* I shrugged and passed the chips. Robin was small with lots of bushy red hair; she had a scar beneath her nose where a harelip once had been, and if you looked at her too long she looked away. Barbara kept cleaning her toes and didn't speak.

Then Robin coughed and I looked up and Reverend Jacks was in the room. He looked at the ceiling and the floor, maybe hoping he could bless something or set up an altar. "Hello, girls," he said, and Robin threw me another look. This time it said, *I can't believe his eyes*, and I had to agree. They were sinful and green, a color to die in and be happy while you died. He took some chips and went upstairs.

Theresa and Morgan came at the same time. Or actually, Theresa came downstairs and spotted Morgan by the door. Morgan didn't go to the front and ring the bell, but stood at the porch door in the grass, looking in through the screens at us. I felt like an insect in a jar. There was no way to tell, but it seemed she'd probably been there quite a while. She was wearing camouflage pants with a shirt and tie and the huge gold Timex on her arm.

No one asked her in, but once we saw her she opened the door and stepped inside. The porch floor was covered with AstroTurf-like carpet, and Morgan's shoes slid back and forth across the pile.

We sat around and listened to the radio until it got dark, and then Robin took a bottle of Jim Beam full of lemonade from her suitcase and passed it around. Theresa had a pack of Newports and we all lit up and watched Robin practice blowing smoke rings by the door. We talked about which of the high-school girls was pregnant, and when Barbara was out of the room, we poured fruit cup in her bra and put it in the freezer. We could see the moon through the screens of the porch.

"I thought we were supposed to have a séance," Robin said.

Theresa shrugged.

"Meet some ghosts and stuff like that."

I lay in my sleeping bag, perfectly still.

"They got in trouble," Barbara said. "They're not allowed to do that stuff anymore."

"All I know," Robin said, taking a razor from her bag, "is that I was invited to a séance." She pushed her nightgown above her knees and gently pulled the razor from her ankle up her calf. Her legs were freckly and white. "I heard Theresa could talk to spirits," she said, blowing the hairs off the razor onto the carpet. "I heard she could walk up the walls and onto the ceiling, upside down."

Barbara guffawed.

"I can levitate if you want," Theresa said. "Who knows the words?"

"Theresa, maybe we shouldn't," I said.

Robin put her razor away. "Who's the lightest? We'll try the lightest person first."

Theresa looked at me. I felt my stomach do a turn but Barbara said, "Frieda can't float in a pool. Morgan's smaller."

"She's asleep," Theresa said.

"I'm not asleep." Morgan put on her glasses and sat up. There was a minute's worth of space. We heard the crickets under the forsythia bush outside.

"Do you want to try levitation?" Robin asked.

"I don't know how it works," Morgan answered. "I don't think I've seen it done."

I thought of the crickets' tiny wings, the arc of gold like a flowered roof above their heads.

"Tell her how it goes." Theresa kicked me in the knee. Morgan wiped her glasses on her shirt.

I explained levitation as well as I knew how: by concentrating hard enough and emptying your mind of impure thoughts, you could float above the earth like a balloon. "You have to believe it, though," I said. "If you have doubts, it doesn't work."

"What does it feel like?" Morgan asked.

I had to think. "It feels like being in different places all at once. Like being in water, with the rest of the world around you floating by."

"I'd like to try that," Morgan said. We cleared a space and she lay down.

Theresa lit the candles and set them in a circle on the floor. She turned the light off in the hall.

"I'm not in on this," Barbara said, taking a seat on the couch. I sat at Morgan's left hand, and Robin sat on her other side. Theresa crouched at Morgan's head. The candles were all around us, casting enormous shadows on the wall.

"There aren't really enough people," I said.

"Of course there's enough." Theresa eyed me in the dark. I could see the outline of her nightgown where it puckered at the wrist. "Should we begin?"

The idea was to tell a story about the person lying down. In the story the person was supposed to die, so that she would think of herself as an empty space, hollow and light like the carcasses of locusts on the trees. When she detached herself from her body, she would rise, or at least the people at her sides could lift her easily from the floor.

Theresa leaned over Morgan's face. Her hair fell like a curtain, touching Morgan's cheeks and neck and arms. For an instant they looked affectionate, Theresa massaging Morgan's temples as she talked.

"Morgan Elizabeth Rausch. Are you with us?"

"I am here," Morgan said. Robin looked at me and laughed.

"It was late at night." Theresa used her otherworldly voice. "Morgan was in her bedroom, doing homework after school."

"After school," I repeated, and Robin repeated it again. Barbara sat smoking on the couch.

"She had a feeling there was someone in the house. She felt a breeze. She went to the top of the stairs and heard the front door open wide."

"Open wide," I repeated.

"Burp with pride." Barbara snorted out a laugh.

"A man with a knife walked in," Theresa said. "And there were bloodstains on his hands. Morgan screamed."

"Screamed," I said.

"And then her father came into the room."

No one repeated a word.

"This was before he was dead," Theresa said. "He was still around. The man with the knife lined them up against the wall. He cut a line in the wallpaper between Morgan and her dad. Then he asked them who he should kill. He said, 'I'm going to kill one of you, and you have to decide which one. I'll let the other person go.' "

My fingers were numb. I prodded Morgan once, hoping she'd get up and walk away, roll up her sleeping bag and go. But Morgan lay still.

"The man with the knife said he'd give them another minute but they had to choose. It was one or the other. He sharpened the knife on a stone. Then he looked at his watch and the time was up so he turned to Morgan's dad."

No one moved.

"And Morgan's dad walked out of the room, and the man stabbed Morgan in the chest and then she died." Theresa took her fingers from Morgan's temples; she arched her back and pushed her hair behind her, then let it fall.

Morgan let out a breath. The bushes were scratching on the screens.

"She was stiff as a board," Theresa said, clearly not interested anymore, "yet light as a feather."

Barbara mumbled from the couch: "Stiff as a horse, fat as a gator," but no one laughed.

"On the count of three," Theresa said, "we will lift her. One. Two. Three."

On three we stuck our fingers under Morgan's father's shirt and tried to lift. Morgan seemed heavier than before. Everyone groaned.

"Oh, well." Theresa stretched like a cat and yawned.

The rest of us stayed where we were, waiting for something, waiting at least for Morgan to get up. She stayed on the ground. The candles threw a yellow light across her face.

"Morgan," Robin said. "You can go to bed."

Morgan didn't move.

We tried to lift her again, thinking she might be in a trance. She seemed to be riveted to the rug.

"I've heard of this," I said. "It's gravitation. People get stuck in chairs and can't get out. You have to break the spell to get them free."

"I'll break the spell." Theresa picked up one of the

candles and blew it out. She should have blown the flame in the other direction, but she was watching Morgan's face, and we saw the wax splatter out, a drop of it landing on the white of Morgan's cheek, below the eye. She didn't flinch.

"She's dead," Robin said.

"She isn't dead." Theresa put her hand under Morgan's nose. "She's breathing. I can feel the air."

"This is your fault," Robin said. "You took your hands away from her forehead. You shouldn't take your hands away before the story's done."

Theresa was pinching Morgan's legs, snapping her fingers next to Morgan's ears. "She's faking. She's a faker."

Robin knelt down and touched the wax by Morgan's eye. "Wake up," she said. "Are you sleeping?"

"Get up now," Theresa said. She found a pin and stroked the arch of Morgan's foot with the pointed end.

"Don't," I said, but Theresa pricked the instep and a tiny drop of blood rose to the skin.

Morgan opened her mouth. She was saying something we couldn't understand. She was talking, but we didn't know what she said.

"Does she know French?" Barbara asked.

I'd taken French after school on Wednesdays and Fridays, and though I didn't know much, just *rouge* and *blanc* and *vendredi* and *chambre*, I knew that Morgan wasn't speaking French. It didn't sound like a language at all. She talked as though her mouth were underwater: it was a garbled gargling sound, a rolling in the back of her throat. She lay passive on the rug, only her lips moving, as if she had figured something out and was trying to explain it to us, calmly and in words we didn't know. It came pouring out of her, all the messages she'd been saving up for years, translated into something that was new.

It seemed we listened there for hours but finally Barbara broke away and ran upstairs. A minute later Reverend Jacks was in the room, squinting and blinking in the light, filling the doorway of the porch in his gray pajamas, his bare chest fatherly and male. Morgan was talking still but the lights were on, and she lay pale and uncovered in the ring of candles with the spot of wax beneath her eye. Reverend Jacks knelt down on the carpet at her side, and Morgan gave a sigh and seemed to pull the words within, speaking to herself instead of us. He passed a hand in front of her face and smoothed her hair.

He looked at the rest of us one by one and we looked away. Then Morgan lifted her arms and encircled his neck. He raised her up and held her to his chest, cradling her knees and back the way that each of us always hoped a man would do. Without a word he opened the screen door with his hip and entered the night without his shoes. We watched them cross the Cooleys' yard diagonally, toward the back of the Rausches' place. We watched the white of Morgan's nightshirt floating just above the lawn. They turned the corner where the peach trees met the sky and disappeared.

· · · · · · · · ·

By the end of the summer, Morgan's mother sold the house, and they moved away. Morgan would enroll in another school, where no one knew about her father or her clothes and where she'd possibly begin another life. Theresa's mother made us go to say good-bye.

Morgan was standing in the driveway near the van,

where some men were tying a pair of bicycles inside. She was wearing a green cotton skirt and a pair of sandals and a blouse with flowers on the sleeves. But she still wore her father's Timex on her arm. "Thanks for coming," she said. "Did someone force you to see me off?"

"You didn't rise," Theresa said. "It didn't work."

I looked down at the driveway, soft and sticky in the sun.

"The rising is internal," Morgan said. "It wasn't visible to you, but I was rising all the same."

"Bullshit," Theresa said, but she didn't look Morgan in the eye.

"You've never felt it, I can tell." Morgan pushed her hair behind her ears. "Both of you are stuck down here for good."

We looked around. The houses were capped with identical roofs; everything looked short and weighted down; our shoes were clinging to the asphalt in the sun.

"What did you see?" Theresa asked. "What did you see when you went up?"

"I saw the future." Morgan climbed to the cab of the truck and let her feet swing out the open door. She was looking down at us in the drive, and from her height above the ground I knew that what she said was true: she'd seen a time when we'd remember her—lying on the porch with a bleeding instep and a message from a world we couldn't know. "You two will think of me one day and feel ashamed. You'll wish you could forget the things you've done."

"What about you?" We heard the truck's rear doors rumble closed.

Morgan was looking through the windshield toward the places she would go. "I won't remember you at all."

dummies

The second time my mother started dying, my brother and sister and I were sent to live with a woman on the edge of town. Mrs. Edna McLeod was a widow who often misapplied her makeup: the dark red lipstick and dots of rouge were slightly out of place, as if she had looked in the mirror, gotten a fix on her features, and then jiggled her head to the left, placing the colors where her lips and cheeks had recently been.

Dan was fifteen, Bea was twelve, and I was nine.

Our parents had wanted to send Dan back to Maywood—an institution—but Bea had fought hard against it, saying that if Dan had to go, she would leave everyone behind and ride to Cleveland on her bike and stay in a homeless shelter there. She said we were supposed to stick together.

My father pointed out that Dan actually didn't mind
Maywood; he had lived there off and on for seven years.

"That isn't the damn point," Bea said. She was just old
enough to swear. Rudeness was a brand-new coat she was
trying on.

I understood how she felt. With our mother sick again,
all of us seemed to be in danger. We were flying apart,
crumbling, with no one to protect us but ourselves.

"When is Mom coming back?" I asked.

"Soon." My father looked tired. He would have to go
with her, but told us the week before that he was sure she
would be all right. But our mother was always dying. The
process took years; for half our childhood she was
rehearsing. Then she was gone.

* * * * * * * *

On a map of northern Ohio you see Toledo to the west,
a small ring of roads around it, and the vast blot of Cleveland toward the east, a tangle of interstates and suburbs
all around. In between those two cities, below the
southern bulge of Lake Erie, you see a grid of smaller
roads, the land cut into perfect midwestern squares by
the cars going north-south and east-west in orderly pro-
gression. The terrain is as flat as a tabletop. If you could
zero in even closer, you'd see that each of the small
towns, marked by a tiny dot, is built the same: cut in
squares and then bisected into smaller blocks, so that any
street with a bend in it is called something like Mount
Curve or Winding Trail. From where we sat, we thought
that getting anywhere should be easy: hang a left to the
redwood forest, hang a right to Plymouth Rock.

Edna McLeod lived on the outer edge of Kenford, about

a hundred yards from the sign that said POPULATION 9,600. Other than the graveyard and the car wash, her house was the last piece of Kenford you drove by on the way out of town.

When my father left us there, forgetting to kiss anyone good-bye, Dan stood next to his duffel bag on the pock-marked driveway and pulled his lip. It was one of those things that he needed to do over and over, as if he thought that doing it long enough would make whatever was bothering him pass on by. We had explained the situation to him more than once, but usually Dan didn't understand what he didn't want to hear. He was sensible that way, Bea said; she said that most people who were smart were really stupid, and that IQ didn't matter next to common sense.

Mrs. McLeod, her fingers bent at an odd angle where they joined her hands, waved at the dust already settling down the road and said that she hoped we'd get along. She shook hands with Bea. (Bea was easy to remember: thin and pointed, like her name, with freckles and nervous hollows beneath her eyes. Most people didn't remember me, on the other hand: I was large and soft, with a regular face—brown hair and no deformities, that's about all.) Then she patted my shoulder and nodded quickly at Dan. People who weren't used to the way he looked seemed to think that meeting his eyes would be impolite. But Dan was very friendly when you knew him. His teeth were pretty messed up and his gums were bad, but he was more normal than people liked to make him out.

"Do you all bathe yourselves?" Edna McLeod's voice was reedy and thin.

I had a sudden vision of this crooked woman taking off

my clothes and lifting me into a round steel tub of boiling water. I stepped back into the shade of a walnut tree. I craved my mother's soft smell, the cool palm of her hand like a magic cup.

"I'll take care of everything," Bea said. Dan was rocking back and forth beside her in the sun. She kept trying to take his hand, but he shook her off, looking down Route 20 for my father's car.

I figured things would probably get even more depressing pretty fast, but then we started toward the house. It was a light brown clapboard, and didn't give a clue from the outside as to what we'd find within.

"Jesus," Bea whispered, when the door was opened and we stood on the threshold with the polished light of September streaming in. On every wall and surface were shelves and cases spilling out plastic flowers, old shoes, ladies' gloves, quilts, pictures, broken kitchen tools, eyeglasses, telephones, crumbling books, ancient underwear, and what must have been the largest collection of Ball jars and thimbles in the world.

Mrs. McLeod closed the door, and I felt encapsulated, cut off from my life as if I'd entered a late-night movie on TV. She nudged a rolling step-stool out of the way and handed me a card from the nearest shelf: "E. McLeod, Antiques and Collectibles." Next to her phone number was a drawing of a jack-in-the-box resting on a stack of books. "I don't sell retail from the house," she said. "I don't want to be bothered. Several times a year I have the dealers come to me."

"Who would want this stuff?" Bea asked, forgetting to whisper.

Mrs. McLeod showed us down a hallway toward our rooms. "The junk of the world recycles itself," she said.

"I'm part of the process. You two will sleep in here, and your brother can have the room across the hall." She rubbed her lips together. They were bright red and made her face look as white and pale as a turnip.

Dan was holding a vase he'd found out in the hall.

"Don't worry," Mrs. McLeod said. "There's nothing very expensive here that can break."

"He wouldn't break anything," Bea said, just as the vase thunked hard on the wooden floor. Dan picked it up again.

I gripped the hem of my yellow shorts so that I'd know where my fingers were. Then Mrs. McLeod put a beautiful pink beaded pocketbook in my hands.

"It's so pretty," I said, touching the shining surface. That was probably why Bea didn't trust me. That was probably one of the reasons, later on, I felt her affection for me vanish into thin air.

. . . .

People used to ask me what having Dan in the family was like. It was fine. A lot of the time he was away, but when he was home, he was always cheerful, and he liked to play almost any kind of game. Sometimes, when Bea and I played marbles or even dolls, he'd come up behind us and pretty soon he'd be hogging the shooter or bending the dolls' skinny legs to conform to chairs, or tucking them into the beds we made of tissue boxes and washcloths. He liked to play with the neighbors' cats, and he raked leaves and shoveled walks for almost everyone we knew. When he turned eighteen, he was going to move to a different school, to a place where he could learn to have a job.

Even though we liked having Dan home, I'm not sure we knew our brother well. In his own way he was private, and what he liked best was to lie on the couch and have my mother comb his hair. Bea liked to pretend that she and Dan were very close, but I don't think they were. He had gone away from home when she was five. She said she remembered playing with Dan when they were kids, before I was born, and that they grew up together. But I don't think Dan remembered that. Bea and I were close instead. Only when Dan came home again, two months before our mother went away, did my sister suddenly seem to love him best.

. . . .

On our first full day at Mrs. McLeod's, Bea made a point of explaining Dan's routine. While he was brushing his teeth (noisily) in the bathroom, Bea explained that, during the time she and I were in school, Dan would probably like to stay outside if it was sunny; that he liked peanut butter for lunch; and that he would walk to the old bus stop near our house to meet us, because he was used to it and it was something he liked to do. She had warned me the night before that we would not get off the bus near Mrs. McLeod's, because Dan would get confused.

"I think I should keep him here." Mrs. McLeod had set out a breakfast of mandarin oranges, hard-boiled eggs, toast, and black sugared coffee, which would make Bea shake until afternoon.

"What do you mean, 'keep him'?" Bea asked. "He's fifteen."

"He may not know the route from here. It's quite a bit farther."

"It *is* pretty far," I said, because my legs got tired after school.

Bea acted as if I hadn't spoken. She looked toward the open cupboards and kitchen shelves, which contained the largest collection of unmatched dishes I had ever seen. "The way is straight. All you have to do is point him in the right direction."

Dan came in to show us his teeth, most of which overlapped one another and were hard to clean. Usually he stuck the end of the toothbrush in his mouth and stretched his lips away from his gums, but today he was shy, or maybe nervous, so he made a kind of grin instead. The belt on his pants was wrong side out.

"Good job," Bea said, repeating what our mother and father said at home. She seemed to have aged ten years in just a day. She had smoothed her hair with water and fastened it into a red barrette. To Mrs. McLeod she said, "I'll take the responsibility."

"You don't have the responsibility." Mrs. McLeod spoke softly. "Your parents have given that to me." She looked at my watch. "That's an old-fashioned piece. It's almost time for you to go."

"Dan will meet us whether you want him to or not," Bea said.

Mrs. McLeod looked at my sister. Bea was pinched, narrow, as if someone had been squeezing her all her life. "I'm sorry this is hard for you," she said.

I helped Dan spread butter on his toast. His fingernails were a mess; no one had clipped them.

"It's not hard for me," Bea said. "I'm used to it now."

Mrs. McLeod sipped her coffee. I wondered whether she had ever been pretty: she had watery blue eyes and a square forehead, and a lacy pattern of veins on either side of a delicate nose.

We picked up our books and said good-bye to Dan, who was looking down at his toast so intently that he didn't even seem to hear. On the way to the bus stop I was relieved to be alone with Bea. I realized I had been waiting for a chance to cry ever since we had said good-bye to our mother on the porch and I had put my face against her dress and tried to memorize her smell. I had lost it already. I thought I could keep her alive by remembering her smell. Bea looked at my wrinkled dress and my ugly brown shoes and said that if I wanted to cry, I could walk alone, that she had had enough crying to last for the rest of her life. That afternoon Dan was waiting for us as usual, happy to carry our books and walk us home.

＊ ＊ ＊ ＊ ＊ ＊ ＊ ＊

At dinner that night we sat down at the table, reached for our napkins, and found on our plates an elaborate meal: brown rice cooked in gravy; carrots glazed with honey and wild herbs; and four miniature birds, one for each of us, nestled in the center of our plates. Bea and I stared at the birds in astonishment. It was like having a three-inch cow appear on your plate, or sitting down to a pig small enough to fit inside a drinking glass.

Mrs. McLeod had clearly dressed for the occasion, with a clean white apron and a cameo on a chain around her throat. Her white hair was curled like a private garden; orange lipstick overflowed the small perimeter of her mouth. It occurred to me that usually she was lonely.

"Excuse me," Bea said. "Could you please tell me what

these are?" She touched a bird with the back of her spoon.

"Cornish hens." Mrs. McLeod severed a two-inch leg from the tiny creature on her plate. She wielded her knife with a butcher's skill.

Bea looked at Dan, who was staring down at his plate with enormous eyes. He'd had a pet parakeet once.

I felt a cool and steady nausea creep from my stomach to my chin.

"I don't want to offend you," Bea said, "but I really doubt we're going to eat these."

"Are they tough?"

At home we usually ate fish sticks, hamburgers, casseroles, spaghetti, and other things whose origins didn't so clearly show.

"We just can't eat them, that's all."

Dan pushed the bird off his plate and made a tent for it with his napkin. He ate his rice and carrots with a serving spoon. When he was done, he scraped back his chair and went to the den to watch TV. He seemed to scowl at Mrs. McLeod. Bea had asked him to say "Thank you," but he probably forgot.

We had a hard time thinking of anything to talk about. The three of us in the cluttered kitchen were a small Bermuda Triangle: anything dropped in the midst of us would be lost, would disappear. Bea shoveled her bird aside with a tarnished fork.

"Tell me," Mrs. McLeod said, "what do you two want to be when you grow up?"

I said "A dog trainer" right away, because I loved dogs and because I was not allowed to have one. Bea shook her head. She hated to be asked that question by adults.

"Bea wants to live in a city," I said. At home, when Bea

and I talked in our room at night, she used to whisper her plans to me. She hated Kenford and hated Ohio, where there was never anything new; she was going to move to New York when she was eighteen. She would live in an apartment and wear her hair long, and when she walked down the street, people would think she was someone famous. But she would be a veterinarian and a stewardess—all our parents' friends would be amazed. I would visit her from Ohio, and the two of us would eat in restaurants every night.

"Alice doesn't have the slightest idea what I'm going to be," my sister said. She drank her milk and asked for more. She had told Mrs. McLeod that we had to have milk with at least one meal.

I looked at my plate, which had pictures of little Dutch people in hats holding hands around the rim.

"I might run a group home for retarded adults," Bea said. "Maybe in town." She ate a tiny mouthful of rice and a miniature carrot. "You know, if things don't work out here, we could probably stay with my friend Carla's family. The Strommens."

Mrs. McLeod nodded. "I know Bill Strommen well. He's an alcoholic. I suspect he abuses his wife." She wiped her mouth and pointed out that three extra children to feed was a lot. "And then there's your brother." She looked up, her eyes filmy and light, searching for Bea's.

"My brother's fine," Bea said.

Mrs. McLeod looked down the hall to the den where Dan was watching TV. "He didn't touch what I made him for lunch. I think he imagines it's my fault your parents are gone."

"I think he probably wasn't hungry," Bea said. "He's really fine."

Mrs. McLeod leaned over her food to be closer to Bea. "Whether your brother is fine or not, you aren't to blame. Blame is only destructive. Why don't you try the Cornish hen?"

Bea opened her mouth and closed it. Then she picked up the bird on her plate in a paper napkin and slammed through the door. My stomach was rumbling, but I didn't move.

Mrs. McLeod had her back to the picture window by the sink and couldn't see Bea head toward the compost heap in the back. But I watched my sister take her dinner spoon from her pocket and begin to dig with it, the small bird next to her on the ground.

"Explain to me what she's doing." Mrs. McLeod reached for the gravy.

"Digging," I said, feeling the tears inexplicably start in my eyes.

"Oh." Mrs. McLeod poured some gravy over her bird and then over mine. She sliced the meat from the carcass on my plate and cut it all into little pieces, putting the skeleton on the counter at her side. The food looked good. "Your sister's a very bright girl, Alice."

"I guess so," I said. I tried the meat; it was tangy and chewy. I wondered if Mrs. McLeod was a kind of good witch, who could cure you with her magic cooking powers. "My mother says she needs to apply herself."

"That's true. It isn't right to spurn a gift. I don't like to see people sacrifice themselves. Does she have very many friends?" Mrs. McLeod put the largest of a basket of muffins on my plate. Bea was skinny and I was round, but I always thought of our shapes as givens—our job was to maintain them, good or ill. I added butter.

Bea was still crouching in the yard; digging with a spoon must have been hard work.

"No, not many. Not anymore."

Outside, it was getting dark.

"Sickness like your mother's is a challenge." Mrs. McLeod leaned over and put her cool, dry, powdered cheek on mine. I thought she would whisper to me some secret, some way of getting through the weeks to come. But she said, "Your sister is struggling; you can help her," and pulled away again.

When she excused herself from the table and left the room, I stood by the window eating leftovers from the pots—the sticky rice with too much pepper, and the buttered carrots with flecks of basil clinging to their sides— waiting for my sister to come in out of the dusk and tell me the ways in which I could help her, and when, and how I could lift the burden she'd taken on.

．．．．．．．．

When our parents called that night, we were already in bed, so Mrs. McLeod answered the telephone in the hall. Bea and I lay in the four-poster double bed in the guest room, looking up at the ceiling and hearing a report about our day. Mrs. McLeod even told them about the hens. She didn't say anything incriminating about Dan.

Bea lay as still as a rock.

"Shouldn't we get up and talk to them?" I asked. I was half asleep, but I could imagine the feel of my mother's hand in the dark, her long nails parting the hair at the nape of my neck. She owed it to me to stay alive, and I'm ashamed to admit that I used to bargain with God about how long I would need her: until the end of elementary school, or until I turned fifteen, or until I married, or until I had a daughter of my own.

Bea said I could make my own decision about whether I wanted to talk to them. She sounded choked, as if she were smothering.

I looked at the collection of things on the wall: colored glass bottles, boxes marked "gloves" and "antimacassars," and books with the bindings gone. Then, just as Mrs. McLeod knocked softly on the bedroom door, I saw the small white statue: two girls holding hands, swinging and pulling each other in a circle, their white porcelain skirts flared out, their heads tilted toward the sky. It had been our grandmother's once. She kept it on her dining-room table until she died. I almost pointed it out to Bea, but she had probably already seen it. Why would our parents have given it away?

"If you don't talk to them, I won't either," I said. "I think we should go together."

Bea turned over. "It's not like that anymore. You have to decide things on your own."

Slowly I put my feet on the cold wood floor. Mrs. McLeod hung up the telephone in the hall.

. . . .

On Saturday morning Mrs. McLeod said she needed our help on an errand in Bastion, ten miles away.

"I'll stay here." Bea was working on a puzzle she had brought from home.

"No, I need you all to come." Mrs. McLeod was rubbing lotion on her hands, over and around the swollen knuckles. "Is your brother still in bed?"

Bea looked at me quickly. We had gone into Dan's

room before breakfast and found the sheets and blankets off the mattress, the mattress off the bed, and his clothes on the floor. We'd picked them up while he stared at himself in the mirror. Bea said she wasn't going to leave him anymore to go to school.

She unbuttoned Dan's pajamas and helped him get dressed. I didn't like to see him even partly naked, with his underwear loose around his thighs. Bea put his legs into jeans and said, "Stand up and zip, Dan," and he did.

I said that Mrs. McLeod wouldn't let anyone skip school.

"I might just be sick," Bea said. She pulled a shirt over Dan's head and he said "Bitch." I had never heard him swear.

Bea turned on me before I could say a thing, her narrow face like a needle. "Mind your own business, Alice. Come on, Danny, stand up." She used our mother's voice to talk to him, and someone else's voice to talk to me.

Now, finally, Dan walked into the kitchen, his hair standing straight up on his head. He was pulling his lip again.

"Daniel." Mrs. McLeod spoke slowly and distinctly. "We're going to drive to Bastion on an errand."

"He isn't deaf," Bea said.

When I asked what we were going to buy, Mrs. McLeod said she'd rather we be surprised.

• • • • • • • • •

By ten o'clock we were riding in the back of a pickup truck toward town. Mrs. McLeod sat alone inside the cab, her head barely clearing the steering wheel, and Bea and

Dan and I rode in back, our legs straight out in front of us like two-by-fours.

It was cool in the back of the truck, and we bounced along on the metal bed over the potholes, which hadn't been repaired for years. Riding backward we saw the things you usually see on small Ohio roads: animals flattened into disks, mobile homes, the blue sky like a lid about to open up above. The pavement rolled beneath us, uncurling under the wheels as we jounced along. Dan seemed better now that Bea and I were with him. We closed our eyes when the sun turned a corner and suddenly faced us; Bea kept hers shut even when we got to town.

The three of us stayed in the back of the truck while Mrs. McLeod walked in the service entrance of Eugene's, the only department store in Bastion. Dan smiled as soon as she left, looking happy, his old self. He stood up and jumped out of the truck. He could be unexpectedly graceful. "I can lift it," he said, too loud. In the past six months his voice had gotten low; because he didn't talk very much, his voice was always surprising when it came out.

"Maybe you can," Bea said.

"Watch, Bea." He yelled, "Alice!"

We watched. He hunkered down by the tailgate, red in the face, the cords in his neck stretching out to make him look webbed.

Bea turned to face me. "It could be she's mean to him," she said.

"Mean to who?"

"To Dan. That could be the reason he's upset. How do we know what she says to him when we're at school?"

"She wouldn't be mean to him," I said.

Bea chewed her nail. Her hair was as straight and stiff as straw. "We don't know that. He doesn't like her, anyway."

I stood up and checked on Dan, who was head-down in effort, the sweat making a path down the back of his neck. I touched him. "It's too heavy," I said. "That was good."

He spat on the ground.

"We didn't ask you to lift it," Bea said. "Don't spit."

He held up his open palms. At the best moments, outdoors, when there was happiness in his face, I could picture him as a handsome grown man. His hands were dented where he'd hooked them beneath the truck.

I looked back at Bea, crouching behind her knees and elbows. It occurred to me that maybe she was afraid of growing up. Maybe she didn't have enough faith in Dan and me.

"I think everything's going to work out," I said, hopefulness coming over me like a breeze.

Mrs. McLeod was waving to us from the entrance of Eugene's.

"I don't see why you suck up to her," Bea said.

I waited, even though Mrs. McLeod was calling. I wanted Bea to know that I would stick by her; I would be like one of those birds that mates for life. "She's taking care of us," I said.

"She's being paid."

Dan had run up to Mrs. McLeod and run on back, feet clomping in his heavy shoes. He climbed up the tailgate and grabbed my wrist, bringing his face too close to mine—Bea and I had given up trying to teach him how far away you were supposed to stay from someone else. "Dummies!" he yelled. At first I thought he was yelling at me, or insulting Mrs. McLeod and Mr. Buehl, the Saturday manager, who was now wheeling a large cloth bin through the parking lot. "Dummy" was a word my mother didn't allow at home. But Dan was pointing at the bin. *Mannequins.* Soon Dan and Mr. Buehl were tossing nearly a dozen life-size dummies into the truck with us, some of them whole, some of them missing heads or limbs, and all of them singed or charred and smelling of the fire that had nearly destroyed Eugene's six months earlier. Most were naked and lay obscenely spread around us in the truck, impassive faces hard against the metal floor.

Bea curled up against the cab. When the truck started, she pulled her sweater up to her eyes as though anyone on the street would notice one pale girl, hunkered down, amid the stack of naked figures and the crooked-toothed boy, standing, laughing, and waving at the passersby.

· · · · · · · ·

At first we played with the dummies out of boredom, and because Dan was always with them when Bea and I got out of school. (Dan had still been asleep when it was time to leave on Monday, so Bea lost her nerve and walked to the bus with me.) We'd drop our books and head for the garage, separate from the house and out of hearing of Mrs. McLeod. The dummies were always waiting, sitting patiently on the cold cement floor in a careful row. They seemed to need us, and each of us had our favorite. Bea adopted a frail bald girl with a wire waist, and with breasts that pointed upward toward the sky. She was blackened on the arms and legs, but she was intact. She looked off to the side, so no matter which way you turned her, she refused to meet your eyes.

I chose a woman who was more in need: she was missing an arm below the elbow and one of her legs was twisted, so she couldn't stand up straight—she leaned forward, as if stumbling, or as if trying to catch up to someone in front of her to hear what they said. I liked her better for the game leg and the missing arm; I imagined her coming to life, needing me to help her through crosswalks, leaning on my shoulder with the stump of her arm. I named her Louise. Dan singled out the smallest of the dummies, a four-foot sexless child with a missing chin. He clearly loved it, and I let him dress it in my clothes as long as he gave back whatever I wanted to wear.

Dan worked hard cleaning the dummies. He washed each mannequin scalp to toe, methodically wiping off the grime with a washcloth dipped in water and lemon soap. He was serious: he washed the eyes and stiffened lashes as though expecting the rigid dolls to come to life, to wrap their arms around his neck and call him Prince Charming, Rescuer Divine. He didn't talk to us anymore. After inserting arms into sleeves and legs into pants he took a comb from the pocket of his shirt and smoothed the sticky, matted hair. Bea and I watched him arrange the hairstyles with his hands, sometimes licking the tips of his fingers to pat a wayward section into place. The dummies seemed to be getting ready for something. The ones he'd worked on looked like conservative farmers, neatly groomed.

One day, when Mrs. McLeod moved his favorite dummy so that she could get a shovel for the garden, Dan stood up and hit her in the eye. Bea and I went to check on her in the kitchen and found her sipping a glass of wine.

me, or insulting Mrs. McLeod and Mr. Buehl, the Saturday manager, who was now wheeling a large cloth bin through the parking lot. "Dummy" was a word my mother didn't allow at home. But Dan was pointing at the bin. *Mannequins.* Soon Dan and Mr. Buehl were tossing nearly a dozen life-size dummies into the truck with us, some of them whole, some of them missing heads or limbs, and all of them singed or charred and smelling of the fire that had nearly destroyed Eugene's six months earlier. Most were naked and lay obscenely spread around us in the truck, impassive faces hard against the metal floor.

Bea curled up against the cab. When the truck started, she pulled her sweater up to her eyes as though anyone on the street would notice one pale girl, hunkered down, amid the stack of naked figures and the crooked-toothed boy, standing, laughing, and waving at the passersby.

* * * * * * * *

At first we played with the dummies out of boredom, and because Dan was always with them when Bea and I got out of school. (Dan had still been asleep when it was time to leave on Monday, so Bea lost her nerve and walked to the bus with me.) We'd drop our books and head for the garage, separate from the house and out of hearing of Mrs. McLeod. The dummies were always waiting, sitting patiently on the cold cement floor in a careful row. They seemed to need us, and each of us had our favorite. Bea adopted a frail bald girl with a wire waist, and with breasts that pointed upward toward the sky. She was blackened on the arms and legs, but she was intact. She looked off to the side, so no matter which way you turned her, she refused to meet your eyes.

I chose a woman who was more in need: she was missing an arm below the elbow and one of her legs was twisted, so she couldn't stand up straight—she leaned forward, as if stumbling, or as if trying to catch up to someone in front of her to hear what they said. I liked her better for the game leg and the missing arm; I imagined her coming to life, needing me to help her through cross-walks, leaning on my shoulder with the stump of her arm. I named her Louise. Dan singled out the smallest of the dummies, a four-foot sexless child with a missing chin. He clearly loved it, and I let him dress it in my clothes as long as he gave back whatever I wanted to wear.

Dan worked hard cleaning the dummies. He washed each mannequin scalp to toe, methodically wiping off the grime with a washcloth dipped in water and lemon soap. He was serious: he washed the eyes and stiffened lashes as though expecting the rigid dolls to come to life, to wrap their arms around his neck and call him Prince Charming, Rescuer Divine. He didn't talk to us anymore. After inserting arms into sleeves and legs into pants he took a comb from the pocket of his shirt and smoothed the sticky, matted hair. Bea and I watched him arrange the hairstyles with his hands, sometimes licking the tips of his fingers to pat a wayward section into place. The dummies seemed to be getting ready for something. The ones he'd worked on looked like conservative farmers, neatly groomed.

One day, when Mrs. McLeod moved his favorite dummy so that she could get a shovel for the garden, Dan stood up and hit her in the eye. Bea and I went to check on her in the kitchen and found her sipping a glass of wine.

"Let's be honest," she said, holding an ice cube to her temple. A red half-moon was rising beside her eye, which was clearly on its way to swelling shut. "I haven't given your parents any real news about Daniel, which in most people's minds would constitute an enormous mistake. Partly I don't want to worry them. They don't need it. But I'm not sure that's the right strategy anymore."

"He didn't mean to hurt you," Bea said. "I'm going to make him apologize." She was pale from not sleeping well, and I knew that she'd gotten in trouble with her teachers at school.

Mrs. McLeod pushed her wineglass out of the way—I wondered which Kenford family had gotten rid of it—and dabbed her injured eye with a paper towel. "I don't care about this," she said. "And I'm not concerned about his etiquette; he doesn't need to apologize."

"He will, though," Bea said.

Mrs. McLeod leaned across the table. "Your brother's a miracle, I know, a beautiful boy."

I had imagined, before this, that once my mother came home, we would visit Mrs. McLeod every now and then and look at the things she had to sell; I would show my mother where I'd slept for three long weeks and we'd buy a beaded purse and look for the small albino squirrel out in back. But possibilities, it seemed, were disappearing. Or maybe they were getting smaller.

"They'll be home in six days," my sister said.

Through the screen door we could see the yellow light of the garage. Dan was sitting there, alone.

"He needs to eat," Mrs. McLeod said.

"I'll get him to eat," Bea said. I'd already watched her, after lunch, tear a sandwich into pieces and put the pieces into Dan, holding his jaw and begging him to chew.

I said I would help. When Bea stood up, I stood up with her. But I wanted to throw myself into Mrs. McLeod's broad lap and wait for the world to come undone.

. . . .

Bea had told Mrs. McLeod that school was closed for the rest of the week for teachers' conferences. I don't think Mrs. McLeod believed her, but she didn't try to make us go to school. We spent our time in the garage with Dan and the dummies. Sometimes he still combed their hair, but at other times he sat with them doing nothing, just touching them now and then: their chipped hands, their starchy hair, the places where they had been injured or damaged or burned.

Mrs. McLeod had a junk dealer in the house—a middle-man, she said—and Bea was afraid she would sell the dummies.

"Ask her not to," I said, looking at Dan. "Tell her not to sell them until we're back home."

Bea rolled a penny on her tongue. Ever since I could remember, she liked to hold things in her mouth: coins, bobby pins, bits of stone. "She makes her money on this stuff. I don't want her doing me any favors."

"I could ask her," I said. "I don't mind."

Bea looked fierce. "No, we'll buy one. We'll ask her how much she can get and then we'll buy one. How much money do you have?"

I wanted to buy a new set of markers and a Frisbee. "Not very much."

"How much?" Bea grabbed my arm.

Dan was sitting on the floor. He was a good brother but he hardly seemed to notice us. He stirred his fingers in the oil on the ground. I could feel Bea's fingers leaving their imprints on my skin. "Two dollars," I said. But I had ten.

At lunch we ate on trays in the garage, because Mrs. McLeod was still busy with the buyer. Bea forced a piece of tuna salad into Dan's mouth and when he spit it out, she slapped him. She and I ate his lunch—she told me I had to finish half his sandwich as well as mine—and then she gave me the empty plates and eleven dollars, telling me to say that Dan had eaten everything.

When I went inside with the dishes and the money to buy the smallest dummy for Dan, Mrs. Mcleod was counting a stack of twenties. The buyer was gone. I saw bare spots on the shelves along the wall. I had dirt and food on my hands and oil in my hair.

"You miss her, Alice, don't you?" she asked, putting her money loose on the counter. I didn't know if she was talking about my mother or about Bea, but I suddenly thought, What if I am the one to move away and Bea stays here? Will she visit me the way I would have her? I put the dishes in the sink and thought of my sister caring for Dan the rest of her life while I lived alone, and I remembered what Mrs. McLeod had said about helping Bea. I started to cry.

When Mrs. McLeod dialed the telephone in the hall, I didn't object. I watched her crooked finger find the long-distance number and I held out my hand when she pulled the heavy black receiver into the kitchen, over to me.

I talked. I had never, I thought, talked so long.

Mrs. McLeod stood behind me, quiet as dust. When I hung up, she rested her old woman's head on top of mine. "Come and wash up in the bathroom," she said.

I thought of the circle of artificial men and women in

the yellow light of the garage, cripples and victims every one. I wished they'd all been sacrificed in the fire.

She ran hot water in the tub and helped me take off my clothes. She handed me a washcloth. I handed her my money.

In only four more days my father would bring my mother home.

. . . .

In the middle of the night I woke up to find Bea putting on her raincoat and her boots, and tucking all of our money—about twenty-two dollars; she had found my ten—into the pocket of her jeans. I got up and dressed as she dressed; we didn't talk. Earlier I had offered to let her hit me, but she wouldn't even answer. Now I was a shadow she didn't try to leave behind. The two of us, in the dark, left our room and walked down the hall toward the front door.

Mrs. McLeod sat in an armchair blocking the way. "I don't think anyone will ask me to babysit again," she said. "I assume you have food, and your raincoats, and some money?"

I nodded, forgetting we were nearly invisible in the dark.

"Good. At least you feel prepared. That's important. It's an illusion, but it can help you through the day."

Bea was staring at the place in the flowered chair where Mrs. McLeod's face was bound to be.

"You girls tried your best. That's what counts if anyone wants to judge you. You were heroes." Mrs. McLeod sounded worn out. The outline of her hair was in disarray. "I'm sure you know enough not to accept a ride with anyone outside of Kenford. You'll find two sandwiches in the refrigerator on the shelf."

Bea stepped around the chair and opened the door.

"It was the right thing to do," Mrs. McLeod said.

We stumbled out.

The air was cool and wet with mist. We got our bikes from the side of the house; I kept an eye on Bea the entire time. I would watch over my sister now.

We rode without looking back. I could hear Bea's breath beside me and the whirr of her gears as they clicked along. Soon the muscles in my legs were aching and my hands were cold in the morning air. I tried to imagine a day when Bea and I would remember our time at Mrs. McLeod's with a sense of fun. Dan would be gone and we would miss him, but Bea and I would be close, the way I had always hoped we'd be. But I couldn't picture it very well. Generally I have found that the future is useless. It doesn't help; at times it may as well not exist. I was stuck on the seat of my bicycle, hearing Bea begin to cry and slow down behind me. I kept pedaling away from her; I didn't stop. Some moments you can't escape from. With the shallow taste of freedom in my mouth, I am still whispering Dan's name on that black receiver in the hall; I am still riding; I can still feel my sister's hatred spurring me on.

infertility

My name is Aaron Bishop, and I have been told more than once that I am a very particular man. Life is short, I have found; the less disorder and confusion in it, the better. An individual day, at its best, should mimic the symmetry and flow that we expect from the revolution of the planets. No surprises, no upheavals. No regrets. My wife, Caroline, left me, which was no surprise to the friends who encouraged her, probably cheered her, as she aired her complaints over coffee at the houses she was invited to alone. I hold no grudges. She had been trying to get pregnant for almost three years.

I had never spent much time with her family nor she with mine, and so when I opened the door of our duplex one morning, about three weeks after she left, and found a man—a boy—sitting on the step, I had no idea at first that he was Caroline's brother. I get up early, with the sun, and the first thing I noticed that day were the thin rays of light illuminating the face of this sleeping person on my porch. He wore thin faded jeans and a flannel shirt, and trembled slightly in his sleep. He breathed with his mouth partly open like an asthmatic child, his head thrown back against the wall. He seemed a poor imitation of some divine, ecstatic pilgrim. His crewcut and his feet were wet with dew.

"Aaron," he said, with his eyes still partly closed. "I came to see you."

I didn't answer. I wasn't sure whom I would be addressing.

The boy had brilliant blue eyes in a lunatic's face: he could have been fourteen or forty-five. He smiled. He sensed that I didn't know him, and assumed therefore some kind of superiority. But looking at that smile, I suddenly recognized my wife. She used it, too—a smile betraying certainty, a curling of the lips expressing amusement at what was taken to be another's imperfection.

Roland was probably seventeen. He was Caroline's youngest brother, a premature runt-of-the-litter kind born a decade later than the rest. He looked as if he'd been raised in a hothouse, like an orchid.

"Why did you come to see me, Roland?" I asked. His family lived in Wisconsin. I was in Syracuse, New York.

He smiled again, shrugging. All the members of Caroline's family are small and thin, but Roland seemed emaciated; he probably didn't weigh much more than a hundred pounds.

Because he didn't answer I let him in, handing him the afghan from the couch. It was early September, but the mornings were cool.

"I'm sure that you know that your sister isn't here," I said.

Roland nodded. "Can I have some coffee?" he asked.

I looked at the clock. Six-fifteen. I usually didn't make coffee until afternoon, when the work at my desk suddenly seemed less interesting, more tiring.

"Or tea," he said. "Whatever you've got."

I made coffee and brought him a mug in the living room.

"You aren't having any?" he asked.

I said I wasn't. "What inspired you to visit? You knew your sister was away. She's up at the lake."

"I know." He looked irritated, as if I were bothering him.

"I'm surprised you didn't call first," I said.

"I lost the number." He drank his coffee scalding hot, the way I drink mine. "Do you mind if I take a shower?" he asked.

I paused. "There's more coffee in the kitchen. I made a whole pot."

"I don't want it," Roland said. After I rinsed out his mug in the kitchen, I heard the water running in the bathroom down the hall.

. . . .

I work at home, on a free-lance basis, as a medical illustrator for magazines. I went through two years of medical school, leaving when my father died and my mother needed medical care herself, and am largely self-taught as an artist, though I have taken several classes here and there. I do consider myself an artist. Though my job is to reproduce faithfully and, some would say, without imagination, I take great pains to instill in my work a sense of the loveliness inherent in the body as mechanism. There is nothing more beautiful to me than the human heart, though my wife has often accused me of being heartless.

I cannot work if I am often interrupted. From seven-thirty until noon I unplug the phone and get my best work done. After lunch I make any necessary calls and run my errands; then I polish the morning's efforts in the afternoon. Roland had probably arrived without any money. In order to send him to his sister, I would have to cash a check, then drive him to the bus station in the hope that there would be a bus to Old Forge, one of the gateways to the Adirondacks, where my family has kept a cabin since 1910. Optimistically, I would lose half the day. It wasn't easy to contact Caroline; we had no phone in the cabin and in emergencies relied on the general store.

Half an hour after he'd shut off the water, Roland hadn't appeared. I knocked at the bathroom.

"Okay," Roland said.

"Does that mean, 'come in'?" I asked, opening the door. Roland was sitting on the edge of the tub with his feet by the drain. He was naked and seemed perfectly dry.

"Did you shower?" I asked. Ronald's clavicles and vertebra were visible through the skin. From the back, in fact, he might have been his sister.

"I'm air drying," Roland said. "I couldn't find any towels."

"They're in the wash. You should have called. There are more in here." I took a towel from the closet and handed it to him. He held it but didn't cover himself at all.

"I don't want to hurry you," I said, "but I assume that you're eager to get to the cabin. You're welcome to stay as long as Caroline will have you. I can lend you money if you need it." I used the word *lend* deliberately, though I didn't expect to get the money back.

Roland turned around, and I noticed that his eyebrows were just the color of his skin. Caroline had always darkened hers with pencil.

"Why did she leave you?" he asked.

"That's complicated," I said.

"Were you cheating on her? Screwing around?"

"That's none of your business," I said. "I wasn't. Maybe you imagine us screaming and throwing things at each other. I suppose that would be romantic. The truth would probably disappoint you."

"Well, I'm ready for the truth," he said, in a monotone.

"I'm sure you are. I'll get you some clothes." I brought him a t-shirt and a pair of Caroline's old jeans that I knew would fit him. She had used to wear them when she gardened, which wasn't often. The yard, unless I took care of it, looked like a hodge-podge of dying flowers and creeping charlie. He put them on. The resemblance to Caroline was increasing.

"So she left you stuck here," he said. "Planted."

"I don't consider myself stuck, Roland."

"Yeah, well, she's up at the cabin and you're in this glued-together building—"

"It's a duplex," I told him. "Use the name. Caroline and I are separated. It makes sense for her to stay up at the cabin; she's between jobs, anyway. Do you know what the bus schedule is to Old Forge?"

"I don't give a flying fuck about Old Forge," Roland answered. I felt the second half of my day begin to disappear.

* * * * * * * *

Caroline and I first met when she was twenty-four and I was thirty-five. Friends advised her, she told me later, that a man my age who had never been "involved" in a serious relationship would be trouble. She found it touching, though, she said—the idea that I had waited, that in some sense I had been saving myself for her. That was probably true. I

never had been in love before, and I fell in love with Caroline
not only because of her beauty and precision (her hands are
as clean and exact and delicate as a surgeon's), but because
of her tendency to look forward, her optimism. I think she
initially approved, though she made fun of, the several
schema I devised for our life together: a given number of
years to save for a house, a given number of vacations, the
approximate date on which our first child would be born.
Caroline was surprised that I wanted children. She wanted
them herself, but she used to wonder aloud whether I would
be able to withstand their noise and messes.

"Look at you," she said to me in the bedroom, when I
picked up her things. "Tidying up, cleaning up, putting
things back where they belong. Stasis is your only hobby.
Why can't we ever let things go? Why do we have to live
in this—cleanliness all the time?"

"You almost said 'sterility,' " I told her, and at that she
started crying, familiar tears.

"Nothing works out the way we want it to," she said.

I told her that she needed to hold on, that things still
might work out eventually.

"I don't want to wait for eventually," she said. A few
weeks later, she was gone.

. . . .

Roland did call the bus station after breakfast. He found
out that the only bus to Old Forge had left an hour earlier.

"Sorry," he said, without sounding sorry in the slightest. He settled himself in front of the TV.

"I'm going to work in my study," I said, hoping he
would keep the volume down.

Roland didn't answer; I wondered how his parents tolerated him at home.

I'd been drawing a series of simple brain diagrams for an encyclopedia—the transverse fissure, the pineal body, the corpus callosum, the optic chiasma—which had turned out well. Illustrators often sketch a cross-section of the brain and head, including a side-view outline of the nose, chin and neck. I went a step further, adding small details to the flesh—the lips curved slightly upward, a more distinct, individual nose, a higher-than-normal forehead. There was a person housing the brain, a person I imagined still ticking and walking, still using that three-pound supervisory center of the body for emotion and thought. I imagined the person as Caroline. I drew her thinking of me, up in the cabin by the lake, thinking she would like to come home and begin again.

. . . .

At dinner that night (I fixed Roland a sandwich for lunch, and brought one for myself into the study), Roland pushed his salad around on his plate and said, "Actually, I heard she left because she couldn't have a baby."

I decided not to answer.

"How come you didn't adopt one?"

I sipped my water. Roland was silent. "That wasn't the only reason that she left," I said. "That was part of it. It added to the stress."

"So you thought of adopting," he said.

I finished my salad. It was six-thirty. I wondered what time I could politely go to bed. "We discussed it."

"Makes you think of a whole lot of Asian kids dressed alike," Roland said. "Is that the problem?"

I got up to wash the dishes. Roland got up to help. "Stay where you are," I told him. "I'll do this alone."

"Dangerous work, huh?" He held up his hands as if I were getting ready to shoot him.

"What's the theory behind your coming here?" I asked. "Are you sent by your parents to cheer Caroline up? Or did they take a longer view and ask you to pressure her to divorce me?"

Roland continued holding his hands up.

"We could call the general store and leave her a message," I said. "She'd probably get it in the morning if she goes there to buy some coffee or a paper." Caroline never bought enough coffee to last more than a week; we used to run out of it all the time. "I don't want it to go stale," she used to say. I dried my hands on a towel and pointed to the number on the pad of paper by the phone. "That way you can warn her that you're coming."

"That's okay," Roland said. "Forget it."

"How about calling your parents, then?"

Silence behind me.

"Jesus, Roland," I said. "Do they know where you are?"

"They might figure it out," he said.

I turned off the water and left the silverware in the sink. "What are you doing here?" I asked.

"I don't know," he said. He had an expression—part stubbornness, part anger, part despair—that I'd come to miss on Caroline's face. There was a poignancy about it that I had tried and failed to capture with a pen.

"Tell me," I said. "Or I'll call your parents."

"They're in Bermuda," he said. "Doing their bourgeois vacation."

If I were a different man I might have put my hand on

his shoulder. "Roland," I said. "What happened? You can tell me. What did you do?"

* * * * * * * *

I have to confess to certain eccentric habits. Caroline used to berate me. "Why does the TV remote control have to be *perpendicular* to the table? Who in hell folds their dirty laundry before it goes in the machine?" I didn't bother to dispute her, but said I would allow her to have her own unusual habits as long as they didn't interfere with mine. "You're my eccentric habit," she said to me once.

An unspoken habit that I never confessed to her is this: after observing a person's character I often imagine what internal organ they would correspond to, what their physical function within the human body would be. Caroline I imagined as the vestibule of the inner ear, the labyrinth in which equilibrium was delicately and precariously maintained. I've imagined myself as a kidney, separating salt from toxin, water from waste. So far Roland seemed more difficult to classify: he was a wild card, a lymph node out of control. I made up the living room couch as a bed for him that night, and went to sleep reviewing our conversation, and asking myself what, in the morning, I was going to do.

* * * * * * * *

In the morning Roland had a fever. He had thrown off the blankets and was sweating as though exposed to a tropical sun.

I put my hand on his forehead. "You should have told me you didn't feel well."

"I don't feel well," Roland mumbled.

The thermometer registered 103. I brought him a bottle of aspirin, a cool wet washcloth, and an extra quilt.

"What time does my bus leave?" he asked.

"You can't take a bus when you're sick." I wondered if his illness could be deliberate.

"Just pack me in ice cubes; I'll be fine."

Duly noting Roland's first attempt at humor, I thought of my desk in the other room, the unfinished cerebrum. I considered Caroline's reaction when she saw her brother borne on a stretcher through the woods. "You'll stay in bed. I'll call and leave her a message."

"Do you want her to come here?" Roland asked. "And hover around over her baby brother?"

I hesitated. In truth I didn't want Caroline to come home unless she was ready. Unless she wanted to see me.

"Better wait," Roland said. "If you tell her I'm sick, she'll come. Blood's thicker than water. I'll just lie here on the couch. You can call tomorrow."

I opened the door to get the morning paper.

"Do you have any jello?" Roland asked.

"No. Do you need some?"

"Well, how about juice. And a TV guide."

I went into the kitchen.

"And some crackers and an extra pillow. If they're handy," Roland called.

I brought him the pillow and arranged the juice and crackers on a tray. "Anything else?"

"No, I guess that's it for now." He turned the TV on with the remote control.

"Call if you need me," I said. "I'll leave the study door open."

"Yeah, great," Roland said. "You can call me if you need me, too."

. . . .

It was difficult to work. First, as I said, I don't like interruptions; the TV noise was distracting. And then there was Roland himself. What he had told me the night before deserved more thought than I had yet given it. I had pressed him for information and he had delivered. He had a girlfriend, he said. Laura. At first he hadn't liked her very much but then she broke off with him and he loved her. He loved her so much, he said, that he had burnt up her parents' front lawn and made three hundred calls to their answering machine. He loved her so much that he had sliced her car tires and then set out to find me when the police arrived at his parents' door. We were two spurned men together, though he didn't label us as such. "I still do love her," he said. "But I don't know why."

"That isn't love," I said.

He'd gone to the refrigerator and gotten a beer. He raised his eyebrows in a question.

"But don't ask me to define it," I said. "You know you aren't old enough to drink."

"Then it's very irresponsible of you to keep alcohol in the house when a minor is visiting." He popped the top. I got a wine glass from the cabinet and opened a bottle of chardonnay.

"I still love her but I want to strangle her," Roland said. "You know what I mean."

"I don't want to strangle Caroline," I said.

He rubbed a hand over his crewcut. "There she is up at

your cabin, on *your* piece of property, when *she's* the one who wanted out."

"You don't look good, Roland." I should have felt a responsibility to his family; I should have called them. I may have decided not to do it to prove to myself that I'm a sympathetic man.

Roland finished his beer and got another. "You look like shit, too."

* * * * * * * *

During the years that she was trying to conceive, we went through the standard procedures and tests. Charting her period. Taking her temperature every day. Sperm count and motility. Then the tests got more invasive. Caroline is squeamish. One of the strategies we resorted to involved my giving her daily injections of Pergonal just before intercourse. I was told to practice on oranges, and when Caroline saw me jabbing into the fruit with a hypodermic she started to cry. The first time I gave her the injection my hand shook, which surprised me. Caroline locked herself in the bathroom when our amorous adventure was over and done.

I'm sure she never suspected that I dreamt up our children. I saw their faces. I know she imagined that she craved them more than I did, that her desire to be a mother was more essential, more biological, than my desire to be a father. I didn't talk about my desire. Since our barrenness technically lay with her, within her body, I couldn't openly express the force or extent of my own craving; that would have been blaming her, emphasizing her failure to conceive. In the end, not knowing a better alternative, I let her pine for our children—for our first scheduled child—all alone.

. . . .

Caroline called early the next morning. I had unplugged the phone but, since I'd left the study door open to listen for Roland, heard her voice leaving a message on the answering machine. She had heard from her parents: Roland was in trouble. If there was any chance he had been in contact, would I please leave her a message at the store.

Roland heard it, too. He came into the bedroom where I was listening to the message for the second time. "Your parents are back from Bermuda," I said.

"Yup," said Roland.

"They might appreciate a call."

Roland shrugged. He hadn't been into the bedroom before. He seemed surprised that Caroline had left her jewelry, and that the top of her dresser was strewn with scarves, lipsticks, hair fasteners and other odds and ends. I had cleaned nothing. I hadn't touched it. Dust was beginning to build up among her things.

"What are you holding there?" Roland asked.

I looked down at the drawing in my hand. It wasn't work; it was something I drew between other efforts. Sometimes I doodled smaller versions on scraps of paper, unaware.

"Let me see." Roland took it from me and held it, turning on the light to study it better. By the expression on his face I suspected that, unlike Caroline, unlike most people who appreciated my talent, Roland saw the art behind the draftsmanship. He studied the illustration for quite a while. "What's this part?" he asked.

"That's the bladder." I had shadowed it in.

"That's the womb, that much I know. Whatever the word is."

"Uterus," I said.

"Is this realistic?"

"Basically. It's stylized. I took some small creative license here and there." Together we looked at the drawing. I had begun it during one of the long evenings when Caroline was crying in the bathroom down the hall. Two small ovals east and west, then a pair of wilted tulips, the petals drooping just above the ovals, left and right. The stems of the tulips led to a large, amorphous blob in the center of the page. I had colored it a dark eggplant. I imagined it stark and lonely, asymmetrical, like the continent of Africa in shape.

"I think it's the best of all your drawings—the ones I've seen," Roland said.

I agreed, though obviously it wasn't saleable. "These are the ovaries, where the eggs are, and these are fallopian tubes." With my finger I traced the path of an imaginary egg. It pushed off from an ovary island, traveling east through the Atlantic in a graceful arc, as if following a tide. I lifted my finger before it reached the Ivory Coast. What a cruel distance, I often thought. What an intimate geography.

I stuffed my hand into my pocket. Whenever I looked at the drawing too long I felt an anger like Roland's, a love so close to fury I was afraid to allow myself to speak.

"Why don't you drive up to the cabin?" Roland was still studying the illustration. "It belongs to you. It's yours."

"I can't," I said. I had suggested, when she wanted to leave me, that Caroline stay at the cabin for a while. She didn't like the idea at first because the cabin itself was a sore point: we rarely visited it together. I am my parents' only child. If I do not will the cabin and the seven acres of land it sits on to a daughter or son, it will revert to the Adirondack land trust. I wanted Caroline in the middle of Bishop property like a seed, a symbol of insemination. Caroline probably wouldn't believe me capable of such faith in symbolism, such trust in the interrelationship of things.

"This is her, right here," Roland said. "This is Caroline in this drawing, isn't it?"

"What are your plans, Roland?" I asked, putting the illustration down.

"I don't have any," Roland said.

. . . .

We agreed to wait another day. Caroline called again that evening but we didn't pick up the phone. We were playing cards in the living room. I had limited Roland to one beer. "Call me either way," she said in the message, "whether you've seen Roland or not. I'll be at the store by nine-fifteen."

"I guess I'll call her tomorrow," I said.

"Good idea."

"Do you think you'll want to talk to her?"

"I might."

"What about Laura?"

He shrugged. "I need to stay away from there for a little while."

. . . .

That night I had trouble sleeping. In fact I got out of bed and watched Roland sleep, remembering the nights when I used to watch Caroline as she slept. Even right before she left she slept so easily and well; she glided passive into dreams while I reviewed the things we'd said, revised our conversations and our plans. My nights were full of nervous watching: lives went wrong and came undone, and even as you held your arms out as a net, the things that you loved most were falling through. "Quite a saddle," Roland said, within a dream. I left the light burning in the hall.

* * * * * * * *

The note he left was short. "Thanks," it said. "R." I drank some coffee with my breakfast and waited an hour before picking up a pencil by the phone. I could tell Caroline that I got her message late the night before, that Roland had made up a fabulous story and disappeared before I had a chance to call. But I am not a convincing liar. I could drive up to the cabin, too. I could try to explain to my wife that I am better and more than she imagines, and that her desires are very fervently my own.

The telephone rang. I imagined Roland standing on the highway, sticking out his thumb, the money I had given him wadded up, obvious, in his pocket. I would worry about him from that moment on. That was presumably the nature of children: their guardians were inflicted with worry and trouble, affection and chaos and untidiness and apprehension. As I heard Caroline's voice on the answering machine in the other room, this time high-pitched with concern, I put my hand on the receiver, all my senses flooding with love. I closed my eyes and saw our cabin full of children. I saw myself running up the rough dirt road toward the lovely shelter: I saw my children crossing the threshold and running toward me, imperfect and unfinished as any art, but welcome, welcome.

dividing madelyn

This is what Madelyn's father told her just before bedtime. "Once there was a little white rabbit," he said, tucking her pajama top into the elastic waist of its companion, "a little white rabbit with pink ears and eyes. It was the nicest looking rabbit anyone had ever seen, and it had plenty to eat and a warm nest to live in. But it wasn't a smart rabbit. One day it hopped right into an open field without looking where it was going, and a big gray owl came down and picked that rabbit up in its claws and tore it to pieces. Now you wouldn't like to be that little rabbit, would you?"

"No," said Madelyn.

"That's what I thought," said her father, as he bristled her hair. "That's why you have to be *smart*. You have to be on the lookout. Keep your eyes peeled."

"Did the rabbit die?" said Madelyn.

"Certainly," said her father, and he sent her to bed.

. . . .

Madelyn's father's name was Arthur. He had red hair and loved airports. Once he flew airplanes for the army, but now he was deaf in one ear, which threw his head out of balance, and he had to run a company instead. Madelyn's mother, whose name was Lydia, and who was sometimes blond and sometimes brunette, said that the only good thing about Arthur was that you could find him in a crowd. He was tall and skinny, with big freckled hands, and it was easy to spot his bright curly hair above the black suit and yellow tie he looked best in.

Normally Madelyn lived with both her parents, but since they were trying out a separation they had two different homes. When she came back from summer camp at the end of July, just two months after her seventh birthday, they explained it to her like this: Arthur needed extra room for all his golf clubs, and Lydia had to have another closet. They watched her carefully to see if she would cry, and then they fixed her favorite dinner—meatloaf on rice—and let her stay up for a movie. When it was time to go to bed, Lydia reached for Madelyn's hand. "I guess we've seen enough of Arthur for a while, haven't we Maddy? Now you can tell him to go home."

After that they divided her. She spent weekdays with her mother in the big house in Westwood, and weekends in her father's new apartment. Though Lydia said no one with an ounce of decency would keep a child in Philadelphia, Madelyn liked the new apartment. It had different color blinds instead of curtains, a thick shag rug and a tiny kitchen with a miniature freezer and only two little burners on the stove. Arthur never used the kitchen, because he and Madelyn ate in restaurants. Every Friday and Saturday they would try out a new one, and Arthur would pull out her chair when they found a table. Madelyn could order whatever she wanted, and if she didn't eat her dinner, Arthur didn't seem to care.

If friends of Arthur's came into the restaurant, he would introduce them in a deep, shiny voice. "Allow me to present Madelyn Burns," he would say. "Madelyn, this is my associate, Mr. Needrobins." When the other man was gone, Arthur would sit down again. "Now, what were we saying?" he would ask. Usually he was the only one saying anything. He liked to test Madelyn, to see if she was *sharp*. He wanted to make sure she could find her way out of any kind of problem.

"Okay, you've landed at the outskirts of an Eskimo village. It's 43 below zero, your throttle link is slipped, and the whole cable's coming loose. Two United States senators are aboard, and you've got to get them to the White House in 24 hours. What do you do?"

"Fix the plane," Madelyn said.

"Right," said Arthur. "But first you have to free it from the snowdrifts. What about that?"

"Maybe I could get some huskies to pull it out." Madelyn pulled on a straw attached to a mocha sundae.

"And you know how to drive them?"

"Mush."

"Okay," Arthur said, "now you're out of the snowdrift. What about the cable?"

Madelyn sat quietly. She hated more than anything to disappoint her father, who always said she was ingenious.

"You'd climb underneath her with a good set of pliers and reconnect the linkage, wouldn't you?"

"Yes," said Madelyn.

"Welcome to the White House," Arthur said.

Madelyn's mother didn't often go to restaurants, at least not with Madelyn, but she *did* go to department stores. She went to Lord and Taylor's, Wanamaker's, and F.A.O. Schwartz. The separation was two weeks old when Lydia and Madelyn went out to look for shoes. Madelyn was trying on a pair of brown leather when Lydia came over with a pair in blue suede.

"How about these, Maddy?"

"All right," said Madelyn, reaching for the shoes.

"Not so fast. I want to know if you *like* them."

"I like them."

"Better than the others? I want to know your *preference*, Maddy. I need to understand your *tastes*." Lydia always stressed at least one word in a sentence.

"I like them both," said Madelyn.

Lydia put her hand on her daughter's head. "What lovely hair for a girl your size," she said. "You'll be the envy of your friends. Do you know why Arthur left me, sweetheart?"

"No," said Madelyn, with a shoe of each color on her feet.

"Well then," Lydia said, brushing away a saleslady, "I expect it won't hurt anyone to tell you. Your father, Arthur, I mean, well he may not like ladies anymore."

Madelyn rubbed the suede in different directions and watched it change color.

"Some people feel I shouldn't tell you this—are you listening, sweetheart?—but Arthur may be a little bit queer. Did you hear me, Maddy?"

"Yes," said Madelyn.

"You don't seem the slightest bit upset," said Lydia.

The saleslady wedged her way between them. "My, that's an interesting pair," she said, looking at the mismatched shoes.

Lydia ignored her. "You think I'm neurotic, don't you Maddy?"

"No," said Madelyn.

"Then let's get out of here. Take those ridiculous things off your feet."

* * * * * * * *

Lydia phoned Arthur to let him know that Madelyn was acting strangely.

"I haven't noticed anything," Arthur said, implying that Madelyn did well under *his* care.

"I'm sure she's *thriving* in your little tenement," Lydia said. "But I think it's odd she doesn't ask questions. You know, about the separation."

"You mean you talk to her about it?"

"Well, what do you talk to her about?"

Arthur didn't say.

"Listen, I'm only claiming that a *normal* child would show concern. It's almost as if she didn't care whether we got back together."

"Do you?" Arthur said.

"That's not what we're talking about. We're talking about Madelyn."

"So we are," said Arthur, and then he hung up.

Actually it was nice having two homes. At Lydia's, Madelyn had her stuffed animal collection, her Madame Alexander dolls, and the big white canopy bed with ruffles on the sides and on the top. At Arthur's she had a foldout couch and two erector sets, six model airplanes, and a real hammer and nails. At Lydia's she could play with Suzy, the cleaning-lady's daughter; at Arthur's she played with a boy named Sam, whom she knew her mother would have hated. Sam had dirt under his nails and said *bag it* when he didn't like something. The first time he came over he broke an ashtray and pulled the knobs from the TV. From then on, Arthur made them play in the hall.

Madelyn never saw Sam's parents or found out which apartment they lived in, but every time she opened the door he would be standing out there in the hallway, doing nothing.

"Come on," he said one morning, when she opened the door for Arthur's newspaper. "Bet you can't play catch." Madelyn stepped outside, but left the door open behind her. Sam closed it. He was ten years old and had extra long arms. "Give you a nickel if you take off your shirt," he said.

"Why?"

"It's just a game. It's what your parents do when they go to bed."

"Mine don't do that."

"They have to," said Sam. "If they don't they go nuts. They go to a hospital and get operated on."

"My parents have different beds. They have two different houses."

"Bag it," said Sam. "You want to play or not?"

Madelyn held out her hands. Sam threw the ball at her and pushed her over. Then he punched her in the chest. "You're not worth a nickel," he said.

"Why not?" said Madelyn.

Sam said he wasn't allowed to tell.

. . . .

Living with them one at a time, Madelyn discovered that
Arthur and Lydia were very different people. They did
things differently. Arthur got up early, read two news-
papers, and cleaned his ears with a handkerchief. Lydia
slept late, tweezed the hairs from her armpits, and never
listened to the news at all. And though they used to talk to
each other, now they had to talk to Madelyn. She felt
privileged and adult. "Do you know what impotence is,
sweetheart?" Lydia asked her over breakfast. "It's when a
man gets flabby. He sees a woman and goes limp all over."

"Whatever she tells you," Arthur would warn above his
paper, "just plug your ears and don't listen. Your
mother's a jackal. She'd tear the flesh from a baby."

Everything was going smoothly. Madelyn had toys in
both her houses, a telephone of her own, and two sets of
clothes in each of two closets. Then one warm Tuesday in
August, when Madelyn and Lydia were shopping for hats,
they saw Arthur walking by on his way to the barber. He
stopped and bowed in their direction. Lydia barely
nodded.

Would they like to go to lunch? Lydia straightened a
glove. It was certainly up to Madelyn. Madelyn looked
down at the sidewalk. All right, then, it was settled. They
went to a small Italian restaurant crowded with waiters.
Madelyn ate spaghetti and her parents ordered wine.

"Madelyn hasn't been eating," Lydia said, just as
Madelyn reached for another piece of bread. "I've been
worried about her health."

Arthur looked at Madelyn's plate. "The noodles are
probably overcooked." He swooped his fork down into

the noodles and twirled it around. "How are you going to be a big strong housewife if you don't eat your lunch?" He laughed and pulled her plate in his direction.

"Tomorrow morning," Lydia said, "I'm taking her to see Dr. Fine. Madelyn, eat your spaghetti, please."

Arthur pulled the plate out of reach. "Tell me the truth, Maddy, are you feeling sick?"

"No," said Madelyn.

Arthur dipped into the noodles.

"It's just a check-up," Lydia said. "You could use one yourself."

Arthur coughed at the spaghetti. "Well, Maddy," he said, "besides going to the doctor, what amusing things do you and your mother do?"

"We go outdoors," Lydia said. "Just to make up for the weekends."

The table shook a little bit and Madelyn reached for Arthur's wine glass, just to steady it, but it fell over.

"God damn it!" Arthur said. There was a bright red splotch on the whiteness of his cuff. A cluster of waiters came by with wet napkins and advice.

Lydia leaned her face near to Madelyn's. "Your father," she whispered, "gets *ill* over laundry."

"I just bought this shirt," Arthur said.

"I remember," said Lydia, stroking Madelyn's hair, "when you were a baby and Arthur was wearing his very best suit, just imported. And you threw up all over it. I nearly thought he'd explode."

"I could have killed her," Arthur said. "Should we order dessert?"

"Impossible," said Lydia. "We have a busy afternoon."

Arthur scrubbed at the winespot with a damp piece of cloth.

. . . .

It was only two days later that Mrs. Kibbey came to baby-sit. Mrs. Kibbey wore thick gray glasses and had spots on the backs of her hands. Madelyn ran upstairs to find her mother.

"You'll never guess," Lydia said, when Madelyn entered her room, "who's taking me out to dinner. Go ahead, guess."

"Daddy," said Madelyn.

Lydia sprayed cologne beneath her arms. "He was practically *begging*, Maddy, it was awful. You wouldn't have recognized his voice." Lydia straightened her hair, which was up in a twist behind her head. "Arthur's a strange man, sweetheart. Did I ever tell you what he said to me the very first time he took me out? He said women were boring. Did you ever hear of such a thing?"

"Why did he say that?"

"Oh, you know—the overbearing mother, the spinster aunts, some kind of Oedipal complex, who can say? But I'll tell you one thing for sure," Lydia screwed on an earring, "boredom wasn't what he got from me. That's why he ran into trouble."

Madelyn walked back down the stairs to watch TV with Mrs. Kibbey. Mrs. Kibbey had a bald spot on her head and liked to scratch it with her nails. During the commercials she turned to Madelyn and asked *what* was going on in the heads of her parents?

"I don't know."

"If you'll be very very good," said Mrs. Kibbey, reaching out a spotty hand to touch Madelyn's knee, "they might just stay right here at home."

Madelyn looked away.

"Wouldn't that be wonderful!" said Mrs. Kibbey, and then the front door slammed shut, and Lydia was gone.

When Madelyn stepped out of her cab that weekend, Sam was waiting by the curb. "Your dad says he'll be down in a minute. He's on the phone." Sam pointed up at the apartment and Madelyn saw her father, waving, pressed against the window of the seventh floor. He looked like a long, tall fly against the glass. Sam gave the cab driver some money and stuffed the rest in his jeans.

"Sometimes I hear him in there," Sam said, "like he's talking to himself."

"What does he say?"

"All kinds of things. I've heard him talk about robots, and about a mission in outer space." Sam stepped on a bug with his bare feet and squished it.

"And what else?" Madelyn said.

Arthur disappeared from the window.

"If you want to hear the rest of it," said Sam, "you can find me later, out in the hall."

* * * * * * * *

Arthur drove to the airport restaurant. He chose a table overlooking the runway and ordered steaks. Madelyn's was burned on the outside, surrounded by crust. Arthur chewed and looked out the window. "That's a 727," he said. "Fourteen accidents in 24 months. Twelve emergency landings. You've got to promise me, Maddy, you won't fly one of those things unless it's absolutely necessary. I'd much rather see you in something you can maneuver." He rubbed a hand through his hair.

"You're not eating your steak," he said.

Madelyn stared.

"What did the doctor say? Did he say you were too thin?"

"We didn't go."

Arthur laid down his fork. "I guess you don't realize," he said, "the trouble it takes to put that meat on your plate. Someone had to raise that cow and take care of it. Someone else had to slaughter it and package it, and then it was shipped all the way across the country." He put his head in his hands. "We're going out again this Thursday. I let her badger me into it."

Madelyn stirred her chocolate milk. "You mean Lydia."

Arthur moaned. "I should have said I was too busy. She always takes me by surprise."

"Will you bring her out here?" Madelyn asked.

"You know your mother hates airports. We'll probably have to go for French." He speared the steak on Madelyn's plate and brought it over to his own. "She'd bust a gut, though, if I did it. I bet she'd really blow her cork." He looked at Madelyn. "Do you think she'd really blow her cork?"

"Certainly," Madelyn said, and Arthur chewed her steak and laughed.

. . . .

"It was disgusting," said Lydia, when she came home that Thursday night. "Your father took me to the *airport*. Honestly, Madelyn, I don't know what *drives* him. He's supposed to be a tactful man. He runs a business." She sat on the edge of Madelyn's bed and smoothed the ruffles. The clock said 2:30.

"Did you get mad at him?"

"Me? I wouldn't give him the pleasure. I pretended I'd never seen an airplane in my life. I let him blather on for hours. He has no cleverness, that man, no mental skills."

"Do you want to know what he told me?" Madelyn asked.

"Not particularly." Lydia was squeezing a hair from the inside of her thigh.

"He said if you had to sleep alone much longer you'd need an operation."

"Is that what he said?" Lydia laughed.

"It was an insult," Madelyn said.

"Yes, I'm sure it was."

* * * * * * * *

Arthur was too busy to go to restaurants that weekend. "Impotent?" he said. "I don't think you could have heard her right, Maddy."

"And she said you were fruitless," Madelyn said. "I heard her talking on the phone."

Arthur was sorting laundry and arranging it into stacks. "You shouldn't eavesdrop," he said. "Help me put these in the closet."

Madelyn opened the closet door. "Ask me a problem," she said. "A hard one. Ask me anything at all."

Arthur closed the closet and went into the bedroom.

"How to get out of a volcano," Madelyn said. "I mean a tornado."

"Some other time."

The doorbell rang and it was Lydia. She was wearing a bright gold dress that squeezed too tight at the top. "Isn't this darling!" she said, walking in through the door. "Does Maddy sleep in the kitchen?"

"Have a drink," Arthur said. "If you haven't already."

"It's just *too* attractive, this tiny home. Do you have miniature roaches?"

Madelyn went into the hall, where Sam was peeling up wallpaper.

"Who's that lady?" he said.

"Shut up," said Madelyn.

. . . .

Mrs. Kibbey came over right before dinner. "Arthur thought you wouldn't mind," Lydia said. "There won't be a thing on the menu you'll want to eat."

"I'm not hungry," Madelyn said. "I'll just order bread and water."

"But Mrs. Kibbey's making fishsticks. I can smell them in the oven."

"Fishsticks don't have any smell," Madelyn said.

Arthur looked handsomer than ever. He was wearing a light gray suit with an orange tie that matched his hair. He had an orange handkerchief in his pocket.

"You're so conspicuous," Lydia said. She put a hand on his lapel.

"And you're as subtle as a bee sting."

When they were out of earshot, Mrs. Kibbey leaned over. "You used to be a perfectly nice girl," she said.

Madelyn tore down her erector sets. She threw the pieces in the toilet and watched them glide along the bottom of the bowl. When Mrs. Kibbey finally fell asleep, Madelyn put on her blue silk shorts and walked out the door. Sam was throwing coins against the wall. His hands were filthy and the zipper of his jeans was halfway down. "Show me how to do it," she said.

He pulled her hair. "I give you a penny and you take off your shirt."

Madelyn did, and then he gave her the penny. Later he gave her another one. They were lying down by the closets when the elevator opened. Arthur picked Sam up by the hair, and Lydia started screaming.

"What are you *doing*, Madelyn, what on *earth* are you doing?"

"Bag it," Madelyn said. Then doors opened everywhere, and the separation was over.

rehoboth beach

I don't have a very good memory, but I can perfectly remember the moment when I first saw Donald Hale. He was my older sister's first quasi-husband (she has had several), and since he left—or since she left him—I have mistrusted anyone who I've loved at first sight. I was only twelve that summer; my younger sister, Vera, was eleven. We didn't yet understand that people you think you have a claim on can disappear. We tried to hold onto him; that's why we brought him, under false pretenses, to Rehoboth, why we lied to him and to our mother, and involved a number of policemen at the Delaware shore. It was all an attempt at preservation. Even then, I think we knew that you can't take your losses lying down. We sensed that we would blame ourselves and each other if, in the future, we weren't able to say: we did what we could to keep him; we didn't willingly let him go.

. . . .

It was June in central Delaware, hot and muggy, and to escape some undesirable tasks that our Aunt Theta had in mind for us Vera and I were spending an aimless morning under the deck that jutted out from the back of the house. We were lying in the cool dry dirt that our old dog, Happy, used to favor: we imagined we were communing with his spirit as we lay in the wide stripes of shade, chewing on onion grass and digging holes in the ground with wooden ice-cream spoons.

When we heard our older sister Nanny's voice, Vera rolled her eyes at me in the semi-darkness. Nanny was nineteen and a drop-out; a sweet-natured malleable delinquent, she had eased her way into so many different kinds of trouble that our mother didn't try to keep track of her anymore. She had been gone for several months without a word. Vera clapped a filthy hand across my mouth when Nanny's feet, followed by someone else's, crossed the sea of grass that was our lawn and climbed the three wood steps to pause above us on the deck. We strained our eyes to look up into the sunlight, through the largest of the knotholes, to see who it was.

All I could see was Vera's ear; her head kept getting in my way. "Quit it," I said, propping myself up; and then I saw Donald, his green eye at the knothole, his asymmetrical mouth at the slat just above the spot where I'd carved my name: Phoebe.

"Look at this," he said to Nanny. "Two stowaways. Two little albinos." Vera and I both had hair as white as snow.

"Come on, Donald," Nanny said, her voice a nasal singsong; she opened the sliding door.

He winked at us through the knothole. Vera's breath stopped. "Little underground dwellers," he said. "I'll see you soon."

. . . .

One of the unusual things about Donald was that he had no feet. He had been in a motorcycle accident long before Nanny met him, and his body ended in two slender tapers past the knees. He wore artificial feet that gave his walk a rhythm, a dip and a swagger that was more a matter of style than a limp. He'd had a special pair of prostheses made to look like cowboy boots, and he wore them with shorts and t-shirts around the house. My Aunt Theta said he looked like a pimp. "Partial pimp," he used to say. Vera and I were in love.

Later, Vera compared the sensation to being slammed against a wall: within days of Donald's arrival every plan, every idea and activity we had saved for summer was driven out of us. We thought only about shadowing Donald, bringing him iced drinks on the deck, spreading cheese on his favorite crackers, riding our bikes to the store for his magazines. Why did we love him? He called us pygmies, slugs, nixies, crayfish, weasels, shrimp and voles, but we sensed in his low, deliberate voice an admiration we had never heard before. In Donald's presence we were overwhelmed with our own potential. He dispensed with the usual questions—how old we were, what we studied, what we wanted to be when we grew up—encouraging us instead to offer our opinions on paganism, death, the ethics of medical experimentation, abortion and war. He seemed to have been everywhere—he spoke five languages and quoted Shakespeare and

Thoreau—but he never condescended. We confessed our most private thoughts to him and he listened, nodding, without judgment, drinking his salted bourbon in the sun.

．．．．．．．．

The conditions of Nanny and Donald being able to live at home were that Nanny go to summer school. Our mother, "calm to the point of being comatose," Aunt Theta said, expressed little surprise about the unexpected marriage, only insisting that Nanny earn a diploma by September.

"And," our mother said (she was a lawyer and fond of explicit stipulations), "either or both of you need to find a full-time job."

"Easy," Nanny said.

"Unnecessary." Donald kissed Nanny, and they folded together like a Japanese fan. Vera and I watched. Before Donald's arrival we were not a family that believed in hugging; on special occasions we bumped up against each other with stiffened arms.

"Unnecessary for what reason?" My mother stretched out the morning paper.

"Cripple money," Donald said. "I won a lawsuit. Poor sixteen-year-old on a borrowed Harley meets a wealthy drunken driver." He sat down. "I was a jerk, a stupid kid. In retrospect, it was a very lucky day."

Nanny sat on his lap and poured herself a bowl of cereal.

"Nanny-goat," my mother said, using the nickname our father had given Nanny. "You've got to stick with it this time. *Motivation*."

"I know," Nanny said, licking her spoon.

Vera pulled me by the shirtsleeve into the hall.

"Why do they want to live *here*?" she whispered. She and I had recently come to the realization that we didn't live in a metropolis, but a sheltered town.

"Who cares?" I said. "All she has to do is finish school." We stood in the hall and pondered. Nanny had never had luck in school. But now we would help her, every day. Vera tapped my shoulder, but I was dreaming: the night before, I had heard Donald crawling down the hall toward Nanny's room, his feet left standing by themselves at the bathroom door. I'd heard his knee-pads scrape the carpet, and I knew that each of us lay awake—Aunt Theta downstairs, my mother in the master bedroom, and Vera and I in the bunkbeds we'd outgrown—listening to Donald fumble through the dark, groping his way along the passage with his hands. Nanny later told me that he pushed a chair across the floor, then climbed up to the seat and crouched for the leap to her outstretched arms. I could picture him kneeling there, as if he were praying or preparing to take flight. I knew that Vera could picture him, too. I knew she wondered what it took to make that leap; we had turned over and over in our beds, hoping someday men might dare as much for us.

* * * * * * * *

I helped Nanny fill out the paperwork for the courses she had to study. "Stupid English, stupid math," she said, checking the boxes. "You could probably do all the homework for these classes by yourself."

"No, I couldn't," I said, because I knew that Nanny was sensitive about not doing well in school. I was afraid she would start comparing us, in which case both of us, in my opinion, came up short.

"I don't care," she said. "Other people can be smart. That isn't the only thing that matters."

"Right," I said.

Nanny looked at me. "You're supposed to say that I *am* smart."

"I *am* smart," I said, and Nanny pinched me. I felt guilty that we didn't spend more time together, that I hadn't looked up to her the way she might have meant me to.

"Let's say I finish all this," she said. "I get a diploma and a job. Then what?"

I tried to imagine what I would do when I finished school. "You could buy a house," I said.

Nanny looked at her hands, which were tiny and rough, the nails bitten around the edges. "You know what Donald says?"

"What?"

"He says the only real education is experiential. He says you've got to educate yourself."

"And he says you can't step into the same river twice, either," I said.

Nanny didn't hear me. "Sometimes I wish I was already old so I could look back on all the things I'd done in my life and sort them out. It's too hard to know how to schedule it from this end. It's too hard to know in advance what things'll turn out to be important."

"What was your wedding like?" I asked.

"It was over fast," Nanny said, licking an envelope to seal it.

"How come you didn't invite us? Why weren't we there?"

Nanny looked at me. "I didn't know where you guys were that day," she said.

* * * * * * * *

June and July went well. Nanny went to summer school and Donald seemed interested in several jobs that Vera and I showed him in the paper: we snipped the ads and pasted them to the arm of his favorite chair.

"You don't see anything in there for disabled dilettantes?" he asked, ignoring the ads and building a house of cards on the railing. "Nothing for gentlemen philosophers?"

"How about music teacher?" Vera said. "How about nurse's aide?"

"I don't think they'd want someone with my *weltan-schauung* in a hospital," Donald said.

"How about funeral director?" I asked.

Donald added a second story. "Now you're getting there," he said. "That's more my style."

When Nanny was expected home from school Donald got quieter. He lined up suntan oil and iced tea and corn chips on the little table, and Vera and I knew to go below. Even from underneath we loved to see Nanny step through the door in her white bikini—the one with a star cut out of the fabric on her hip, which made a five-pointed sunburn on her skin. Nanny's hair was white like Vera's and mine, but fluffy like cotton, thin and almost translucent at the ends. She didn't cut it and it didn't grow; it was two or three inches long and framed her face, and her copper eyes, like a nest of dandelion seeds.

Vera and I lay silent underneath them in the dirt below the deck, hiding even though they both knew that we were there. We could have scratched the soles of their feet with reeds or sticks from where we lay, but it was better to pretend to be unnoticed in the grass, enduring the threadlike paths of insects on our legs. We used to imagine what we'd look like with enormous drowsy breasts, hips that reflected sunlight, and toes with lightly painted nails like our sister Nanny's. Whenever Aunt Theta, who got her name because she had studied Greek in college, asked for us, Donald would say, "I haven't the foggiest," while spilling his drink so that it would splatter onto our faces down below.

. . . .

In August I started to worry. Nanny didn't seem to have any homework anymore, and neither of them showed signs of a full-time job. Sometimes Nanny left Donald waiting on the deck, the ice cubes melting to water, the corn chips roasting in their little silver bowl.

"Don't worry," Donald said. " 'He who is in love is wise and becoming wiser.' " The classified ads on the arm of his chair had curled up in the sun.

Vera, disgusted, went to the kitchen for lemonade.

"Nanny's always been a pain in the neck," I said. "Once on her birthday we even—"

"Nope, nope, nope," Donald said. "Enough. Step over here. I've got something that'll broaden your horizon." He lifted the lid on a tiny can and showed me a cluster of miniature pearls, black and shining; he scooped out several dozen with a spoon.

"What are they?"

"Never mind," he said. "Open. You need to be receptive to the world's treasures."

I opened my mouth. "Donald," I said, and the spoon went in.

"Don't deny experience." Gently he held my lips shut with his fingers. I pressed the salty eggs to the roof of my mouth. "That's what I try to tell your sister. The world is waiting." I swallowed. "How can she turn her back on it?" he said.

By the second week of August Aunt Theta was given to sighing in the air-conditioned kitchen. She had found out that Donald was divorced. "You wait and watch," she said, arguing that Nanny would eventually outgrow her affection for Donald as she had outgrown almost everything else. Nanny had a habit of casting off clothing and hobbies and people: almost nothing held her interest for very long.

"They look happy when they're together," I pointed out.

"*When* they're together," she said. "And what does happy mean, anyway?" She sliced an onion. "How long can that last? True love doesn't wear a face like the one your sister's got on. Real love doesn't look like that."

"What does it look like?" I asked.

Aunt Theta opened the refrigerator and moaned. She pried the lids from plastic tubs and discovered valleys in the mashed potatoes, teeth-marks in the drumsticks and the cheese. "He's a cannibal," she said. "Look at this melon!" She held up a cantaloupe that looked as if it had been raked by a lion's paw. "Donald Hale isn't fit to live indoors," she said. "I don't blame your sister for a lack of feeling, not right now."

"What is that supposed to mean?" my mother asked from the other room.

Aunt Theta was shaking her head.

"Say it, Theta, get it off your mind." My mother came

into the kitchen. She was calm but very persistent, capable of waiting all day for an answer to a question.

"What I'm thinking," Aunt Theta said, "is that we don't even know, we don't have any proof, that this marriage is legitimate."

"In what sense?" My mother liked Theta; she valued Theta, who had lived with us ever since our father died, cooking and taking care of the house while our mother worked. But sometimes, she privately explained, Aunt Theta made her tired.

"Have you seen a ring? Have you seen a marriage certificate? Any pictures? Have you seen evidence of a wedding gown?"

"You never asked me for any evidence when you were told that I married your brother. And I got married in a dark blue dress; I never had a wedding gown."

"That was just after the war, Jocelyn," Aunt Theta said. "Things were different."

"As far as I can tell, things are always different," my mother said. She gave me a look full of what might have been pity. "What do you think, Phoebe?" she asked.

What could I say? I thought that if Donald left I would shrink, that it was his presence in our house that allowed the air to fill with oxygen each day.

The phone rang. I answered it and put the call on our brand-new speaker phone. My mother loved technological novelties and signed up for any new service that was introduced.

It was Nanny, saying that she wasn't coming home that night for dinner.

"Why not?" Theta asked from the sink.

Nanny paused. "Other plans. Let Mom know."

"I can hear you perfectly," my mother said.

"Fine. Now you all know I'm not coming." Nanny hated the speaker phone.

"What about your husband?" Aunt Theta asked.

"Yeah, tell him, too," Nanny said.

"When are you coming back?" I asked.

"Later," Nanny said. She hung up the phone.

. . . .

It took me a while to notice that the new way in which Vera was walking was a limp. She ambled. She took long, slow steps with a subtle hitch in them, as if, having been injured and then cured, she couldn't remember whether to favor left or right. She seemed to have wads of chewing gum stuck to her heels.

"Vee," I whispered one afternoon as we lay in our usual places under the deck. Donald was reclining in his favorite chair above our heads. "Nanny's messing up, Vee," I whispered, so quietly that I could barely hear my own voice. "I'm not even sure she loves him." Vera had her eyes closed, but she turned slightly toward me. We were both pale, as sunless as grubs. We had spent weeks beneath the deck, amassing towels and pillows and food in the lee of the house, a cooler and a thermos and a radio.

Vera shrugged. She felt that Donald would love Nanny whether Nanny loved Donald or not; I, on the other hand, felt a sort of doomed responsibility for their mutual affection.

"You know we should be nicer to her," I said. This was an old refrain and Vera didn't want to hear it: Nanny was older and therefore lonely, and she suffered, or so our mother said, from remembering our father before he died. Vera and I hadn't really known him, but the story was that Nanny had been his favorite, and that she had never felt like a member of the family once he was gone.

"Why should I?" Vera hissed, her eyes still closed. "I should be nicer because she'll be twenty before she graduates from high school?"

I rolled over so that my mouth approached her ear, so that the knothole letting a cylinder of sunlight into our underworld seemed to blind me. "In fourteen days it'll be September. I don't think Nanny's going to finish school."

I rolled back into the shade and watched Vera smooth her lips together. She had been quieter lately, full of some unspoken plan. I wanted to be in on it, whatever it was.

"You can tell me what you're thinking," I said. I had a theory that every person in the world was incomplete, and that because each of us were only halves of actual people, unfinished, we held within ourselves an element someone else required to survive. I had shared this theory with Donald and he said he thought it applied to Vera and me.

Vera shifted along the ground so that she lay exactly in Donald's shade. Nanny wasn't home. "I have a couple of ideas," Vera mouthed.

I moved closer, into Donald's shadow. "Let's hear."

. . . .

Vera's immediate plan involved sending Donald and Nanny out to dinner. "Time," she explained, "is what we need most." It was the third week of August. Gaining an extension of the deadline from our mother wouldn't be easy; in general she was completely uncompromising.

I had asked Nanny where she went when she was supposed to be at school. She waved me away and said she didn't know. I wanted to shake her. I wanted to rattle every bone. Instead, on Vera's insistence, I gave up my savings in the guise of a wedding gift, so that Nanny and Donald could eat in a restaurant in downtown Dover.

"It'll be worth it," Vera said. "Generosity—" she nodded toward our mother "—can be contagious."

It was.

Later that week, Aunt Theta and my mother and Vera and I watched them saunter down the sidewalk toward the car. Nanny wore a sleeveless dress; Donald lightly cupped her neck in his hand and kissed her. They seemed happy and romantic; the word "newlywed" seemed to fit them.

"They do make a good looking couple." Aunt Theta sighed.

My mother stared down at the sidewalk when they pulled away. "December," she said, in a private announcement to Vera and me. Four months. The possibilities seemed almost endless.

We ate spaghetti and meatballs that night, the four of us thoroughly cheerful at home for the first time since Donald had moved in. My mother opened a sparkling cider, which we drank in champagne glasses, Vera and I clinking ours together during the meal.

After we finished, Aunt Theta decided that we all deserved hot fudge sundaes, and she dished up the ice cream while my mother washed the pots.

The phone rang. Aunt Theta answered it and put on the speaker. It was someone named Ralph, for Nanny.

"Does she have your number, Ralph?" Aunt Theta asked in a near falsetto.

"Probably," Ralph said. "Is she coming in later?"

"Probably," Aunt Theta said, warming the chocolate in a pan.

"Much later," Vera echoed.

Maybe Ralph had the sense that he was being made fun of. Maybe the speaker phone disoriented him. "Tell me when she's coming in," he said.

Aunt Theta raised her eyebrows. "I have no idea, Ralph, she's married now."

"Well, shit, she was here with me last night," Ralph said. "She wasn't acting married then." He laughed. "Hello?"

Aunt Theta hung up the phone. The chocolate burned to rubber in the pan. "It wasn't truly a marriage," she said, after the ice cream had melted. "It was never love. Nanny just shouldn't have married him; she never loved him, I could tell."

Vera's limp as she left the room was so pronounced, she seemed to stagger.

"I think it's a tragedy," Aunt Theta said. "And personally I feel very sorry for Nanny, I really do."

"Dry up, Theta," my mother said.

. . . .

. . . .

I don't think anyone called it a kidnapping at the time, since Vera and I were the ones who engineered it, but that's how it came to be labeled later on. We had left a note (typed) for Nanny—*Donald has left you. Now you'll be sorry*—and a note for Aunt Theta and our mother, saying that they shouldn't worry, that we had a plan, and we would probably be back in a day or so.

The sky, on the afternoon we left, was heavy with clouds, and the back of Donald's jeep was full of what Vera had stuffed into it: sleeping bags, a tent, a rubber raft, a cooler of food, and our mother's credit card. "Where are we going?" Donald asked when he saw it. It was the first week of September, the weekend after Labor Day. Our mother and Aunt Theta were shopping for new carpeting for the living room.

"Rehoboth Beach," Vera said. "Do you know where it is?"

"Pretty much." We were standing on the driveway. Donald looked back toward the deck. Nanny barely set foot on it anymore.

"Nanny drove down there this morning in Mom's car," Vera said, straight-faced. "We thought we could catch up with her."

We waited.

"Is that what you thought?" Donald smiled, holding his hand out for the keys.

It took only an hour. Donald packed his own suitcase and then we were driving: through small towns, past beanfields, swamps, chicken farms, orchards, flea markets, mobile home parks and houses caving in by the side of the road. Donald looked haggard; he didn't talk while he drove. When we smelled the ocean he parked in front of a country store.

"Why hasn't he asked us where we'll meet her?" I hissed, when he went inside.

"Because he trusts us," Vera said.

"What if Nanny doesn't come home? How can we call her? What if she doesn't see the note?"

"Why wouldn't she see it?" Vera asked, looking away. She seemed aloof, independent, as if we were no longer in this together. Despite our preparations, I suddenly felt we had no idea what the day would bring.

* * * * * * * *

Donald had trouble walking across the sand. His feet sunk in above the shoes; I was afraid he'd sprain a knee until we reached the darker, hard-packed sand at the water's edge. He put down the cooler with a groan.

The beach was nearly empty. There were several day-trippers like ourselves, a dozen fishermen, occasional joggers, and two or three kite flyers on the sand. Even so it seemed deserted. The tide was low; clumps of seaweed rotted slowly in the sun.

We ate some sandwiches and Donald filled three paper cups with bourbon. He had never let us drink before, though we had teased him; this time he poured and passed the cups without saying a thing. I thought it tasted like kerosene smelled; I saw Vera working hard to force hers down.

When it got dark we raised the tent beneath the moon.

For a while we didn't want to get in it. Donald walked along the water. Vera flipped a horseshoe crab onto its back with the toe of her shoe. It was empty and dead, a vacant home. "Who do you think you'll marry?" she asked, filling the husk with bottle caps and shells.

I didn't know. Sometimes I imagined older, bearded men, men in ties and polished shoes, but I always had trouble focussing on their faces. "What about you?"

Vera shrugged. We climbed the dunes to a sheltered

spot. First Vera stood watch while I took a pee, and then I watched while she had her turn. She took a long time squatting there. The sky was black when she finished up.

"Look at this," Vera said, holding a crab's claw in her fingers. Her speech was hard to understand. The hinge of the claw opened and shut. "Let me pinch you," she said. I let her do it. She pinched my stomach and my chest, and I didn't open my lips to make a sound.

Donald was sitting outside the tent when we got back, the open fifth of bourbon by his side. He had lined up three new drinks in paper cups, and I felt ill just looking at the one that would be mine.

Vera fell onto the sand beside him. In a grocery bag she found a sack of potato chips and a pound of raisins. She stacked some potato chips on her tongue and then poured in the bourbon.

I felt there were things we should have done: we should have unrolled our sleeping bags and brushed our teeth. We should have poured the entire bottle of bourbon on the sand. Donald reached for a strand of Vera's hair. It hung straight past her shoulder, lank and thin. He wound it carefully around her ear. She sat rigidly still, her mouth half open the way it looked when she fell asleep.

He leaned toward me and whispered, "Why don't you tell me why we're here."

Vera seemed hypnotized; she seemed to be sleeping sitting up.

"It seems like the right time to address that question," Donald said. "Don't you think so?"

"Nanny's supposed to meet us here," I said. "We were going to call her."

Vera hiccuped.

"She used to really like it here in the summer. We used to come down here sometimes for the day." I realized that it had been years since Nanny had come with us. Maybe it was only Vera and I who had liked it all along.

Donald leaned against the cooler and unbuckled the straps that held his feet. Then he took them off and held them in his hands, like a man in a fairy tale or a dream.

I held the crab's claw in my hand. I worked the hinge: open and shut, hungry and closed.

"We left her a note," I said, feeling helpless.

Donald shook his head, as if implying that there were things I shouldn't know. I was supposed to grow older and find them out by trial and error, by failure and experience, alone.

Vera kept hiccuping. "Nanny's gone," she said.

Donald rubbed her neck with a finger.

"You didn't even notice," she said, furiously, to me. "You didn't see her."

"See her when?" I stared at Vera.

"You were in the bathroom," Vera said. "She had a suitcase. I saw her getting into somebody's car."

"Ralph," I said.

Donald said nothing. He smoothed the hair from Vera's forehead, which made her cry.

"She left with Ralph?" I yelled. "Was it him? Why did we come here, then? That doesn't make sense. Why did we bother to write those notes?"

"*You* wrote the notes," Vera said. "I tore them up."

"So nobody knows we're here," Donald said.

Vera sobbed.

"Nobody knows," Donald said. "Is that what I'm hearing?"

* * * * * * * *

Later, Vera threw up outside the tent. Donald cleaned her off and zipped her into her sleeping bag. With the sound of her breathy snoring in the background he began making shadow pictures on the tent wall. I held the flashlight; he used his hands and then his legs, the misshapen stumps surprisingly agile. When I had my turn, I made a swan.

"Vera's in love with you," I said, and Donald nodded.

He shaped a wolf howling, noiseless, at the moon. We lay on our backs, and until the flashlight burned out, we watched the wolf wail and the swan ascend, and invented several other creatures of our own.

* * * * * * * *

I woke to the sound of Donald dressing in the dark. I didn't move while he put on his jeans and an extra shirt, but when he zipped up his leather jacket I touched his arm. He untangled himself from the sleeping bag and the trash, and handed me a roll of twenty dollar bills. Through the window in the tent flap I could see the stars.

"Don't wake her up," he said, nodding at Vera. "I just remembered that there's somewhere I have to go."

"Are you coming back?"

"That's an emergency fund," he said. "In case you get hungry. I may be gone for a little while."

I watched him through the tent's window. When he reached the dunes he forced his weight from side to side, loping up the sand and pulling the dune grass out in handfuls as he climbed. He walked the way that Vera walked, I thought.

I unrolled the curl of bills and found that all but the outer twenty were singles; we had twenty-seven dollars to our names.

When the sun came up I opened the tent and crawled outside, sitting on the tarp in my nightgown. I waited. Joggers trotted down the beach. Crabs and seagulls did their work beside the pier.

Vera's breathing sounded clear and quick behind me. I knew that this time we would think alike, as we used to do: what did it matter if Aunt Theta stammered hoarsely on the phone, or if our mother, once stoic to the point of obsession, wept obscenely in her morning coffee? We wouldn't call. Together, we'd wait tediously and in constant hope that he'd return, that he'd put his arms around our waists, twine our hair around our ears, graze our cheeks with the edge of his thumb, and offer secrets about the partial lives within us, that could be made whole.

an explanation
for chaos

—You said you were cruel to him. When were you cruel?

I was cruel at the beginning of my life and will be cruel at the end. Once I told him I wished he was dead. And once he reached out to touch my hair, he wanted to comb it, but I ran away.

—Now he's an old man and you regret such indiscretions. He writes you letters.

Yes, yes, letters about 'The State of the Soviet Union,' 'The Problem of Quarks,' 'Proper Uses of the Nine-Iron.' Pages and pages. Descriptions of arguments he wishes we'd have, engineering feats, revisions in the third law of Thermodynamics.

—Your father's a scientist.

Of the worst kind. Expert amateur in every field, a man

with reasons and ideas, inordinate confidence, a terrifying certainty regarding the order of things.

—And your mother?

Generally modest and unassuming, a hater of snobbery and peevishness in all its forms, a bridge-player, brown-haired, barely five-foot-two, a streak of feistiness well hidden below the surface. But she is a shadow beside my father, a subtle firmament, a song without words. She was beautiful once.

—Describe your father.

Physically, a squat and stringy man, a peasant's build, muscles in the calves and lower arms. A few clumps of grayish hair around a fist-sized sunburn at the top of the head. Eyes like blue stones. A buttressed nose. Lips in an expression of disgust. One silver tooth, a wedding band too small for his finger; dark, leathery hands with plenty of callus. Alligator t-shirts and a belt buckle with his initials, RJF.

—His interior is undoubtedly more complex.

Undoubtedly.

—And is this the heart of our conversation? The very center?

My father, yes.

—Discuss the reasons you resent his presence.

At the age of five, for yelling at me to be quiet when I hadn't been talking. At the age of seven, for standing beside me while I played the piano, humming the tune as it should have been played. At the age of ten, for accusing me of lying when I actually *was* lying. At the age of fifteen, for refusing to notice me. For coming home from work in his steel-tipped shoes, ignoring my face and my ideas.

—Your age at present?

Twenty-eight.

—Answer the following question as truthfully as possible. Why did you lie to your father and how often did you do so?

On all occasions and in any climate. On the boardwalk in Ocean City, New Jersey, over a slice of pizza allegedly purchased only forty minutes before supper. In his bedroom in Wilmington, regarding a centipede found flattened against the wall with a black-soled shoe. On the eve of my departure for college, in reference to issues of virginity. At the burial of my dog, Woofer, when asked if I was sad. I always refuse to be sad in his presence, as he refuses to be in mine.

—For this you are firmly set against him, and can't forgive. Is that the essence of our talk?

Quintessence.

—Let's begin at the beginning. Was he present at your birth?

Pacing the waiting room, fatherly, a sliding grin below his nose. I was fifth in a line of daughters, a last resort.

—What did he bring with him?

To the hospital, a cribbage board, intended to entertain my mother in the labor room. To my existence, a series of longings and a vague dissatisfaction, a love of graveyards and a need for affection greater than that he was willing to supply.

—Is this common among Germans?

Cribbage? No, their game is pinochle, mainly, but my mother being English this would have seemed inappropriate, cumbrous, a legacy intended to warp the card-playing future of the eager fetus.

—Tell me about your ancestors.

On one side, Lady Godiva and the Knights of Templar,

a long line of bookworms and opera buffs, even a great-grandmother nicknamed "Mother of Israel" for bearing twelve sons. On the other side a group of scrappy immigrants from Leipzig, old women who refused to allow their husbands a moment's peace.

—Describe your childhood.

We lived in Wilmington, Delaware. In the house I grew up in, there was a bathroom with three sinks, a shower, and two identical toilets side by side. My father designed it with special allowances for pipes and plumbing, so that all three sinks and the tub could be running water, and the toilets could flush simultaneously. It was a joy to watch, and when my sisters and I were children, we often brought our friends to see the bathroom, where, on the count of three, we pushed the handles and turned the small glass knobs, and listened to the glory of the water all around us.

—Is that all?

It was the root of my father's frustrations. Despite the matching toilet paper fixtures, the six-foot mirror above the sinks, the standing towel rack with fifteen arms, none of the five of his daughters agreed to use the room together. Intensely private, we lined up quietly outside, taking our turns and making sure to lock the door behind us. Except for the watery exhibitions, we used the bathroom one by one.

—When you were seven you took a walk and lost your way. A policeman brought you back in his patrol car and there was your father, raking leaves in the side-yard. What were his words on this occasion?

Where the hell have you been? We didn't know you were missing.

—Several years later, he was standing in the very same

spot when you rode your bicycle down the hill and into the driveway, obstinately refusing to use the brakes because your sister had dared you not to use them, and slammed into the lamppost, landing face-down in the pachysandra. What did he say?

He said, *What in god's name do you think you're doing, Alison?*

—You have always resented him. Where does your anger come from?

Not from raw dislike and not from distaste. The best of me was born from him, his love of stories. His unhesitating lies.

—What type of lies?

Of grandparents stronger than they were in fact, of people he wished he knew but never met. He is a tale-teller at heart. He used to creep into my room and pluck the nightlight from the wall; it was darker than ink, he'd drop it deep in his jacket pocket and sit in the rocker at the edge of the room. He'd prop his feet on the end of my bed and tell stories, bloody adventures about men stranded at sea without medicine (one of them removed his own appendix without anesthesia; another tore out his own tonsils, gazing at his terrified face in a full-size mirror), or science fiction tales of black clouds covering the sun, comets barely missing the earth in yearly orbits, exploding stars. *We're so small,* he used to say. Then he'd walk out the door.

—His love of science is what bothers you. It makes you jealous.

Superfluous more than jealous. Redundant. Infinitesimal. I was the worst of his pupils, confusing neutrons with protons, the laws of gravity with laws of friction. The quadratic equation slid through the warm blue ropes of my cerebrum, remaining buried there, wasting space.

—Once, as a teenager, you stood poised outside his bedroom door in the middle of the night, listening.

True, I stood by the door hoping he would open it, allow me to confess to things I hadn't done, a whole childhood full of wrongdoing and imagination. I hoped he would fling wide the door in his striped pajamas, arms open but eyes half shut, and ask me what I had done.

—Were you guilty?

As most offspring are, guilty of craving his attention in any form, capable of sex and other theatrics to win his notice, his bald eye roving the crevasse of my life.

—Define *cerebrum, cerebellum.*

The great and lesser brains, respectively. A convoluted mass of nervous tissue, senseless lump of ugly cells, most of them never put to use. Some dead, others dying.

—Your father is an old man growing older. He dreams of death in all its forms.

Both of us do. I dream of the end of the world as my father's face rising over the side of the earth instead of the sun. He dreams of hospitals, nursing homes, I.V. tubes, enemas given by young black women.

—And you refuse to forgive him?

Not for the anger, but for the love.

—What about love? He never offered it?

Never named it, mentioned it, spoke it out loud.

—Not in twenty-eight years?

Not in my life. Seldom in his.

—Describe his attitude toward tears.

In the middle of an argument he once said: *crying is justified only in the event of the death of a healthy child.*

—Do you ever attempt to see things his way?

Not really, not to any great extent, not at all. He thinks that anything can be explained, that anything studied long enough can be understood.

—And your attitude is the opposite?

That almost nothing has a reasonable explanation, that the longer a thing is studied, the more abstract it will become. But my father explains the origins of air, the earth's ingredients and measure. He describes the solar system as a raisin-crumb-cake: the raisins are planets, the doughy mass a universe of sky. The cake will bake and the raisins will rise. . . .

—What does he fear?

Dissipation and waste. The separation of matter into spheres, the undoing of those spheres, the inevitable movement from order to disorder. He searches day and night for a special logic to destruction, a pattern for all unreason, an explanation for chaos. And only in the darkest moments does he sense a tiny crack, a hair-line fissure through which his knowledge, like a clever gas, escapes when he isn't looking. Vulnerability rushes in to take its place.

—Is this chaos?

A related phenomenon, chaos being its counterweight, its nearest neighbor. The degradation of energy. The tendency of small, otherwise reasonable forces to disagree and move away, traveling in centrifugal directions.

—Define *centrifugal*.

Flying, tending to flee, from center.

—If your father were a comet moving away from the earth in a centrifugal direction, what would you be?

A net of stars, result of some unknown explosion, scattered across the frying pan of night above his head; a warm illusion, white filament, ignoring him as he rumbled toward the edge of my dispersion, looking right and then left with his round comet eyes, his blue-gray craters.

—Earlier you said your father was a scientist. Is he also a star-gazer?

A man of many hats. Physicist, businessman, star-man, hat man.

—On the eve of your marriage, you telephoned your father from the business phone downstairs. He answered in the bedroom but said nothing, and you both held onto the phone in silence. Was that cruelty on his part or yours?

. . . .

—We still don't seem to be covering this question of resentment. Even the grandchildren have forgiven him.

True, they play in his lap. He is accepted, pardoned. He carves the roast at the head of the table, doling patriarchal slices thin and thick on the point of his knife. They pardon him for his age and for his stature. He is guiltless at the head of the table, therefore irresponsible, irredeemable.

—Does it make you uncomfortable to be incapable of forgiveness?

He ignored me. He compared me to others. He refused to encourage me. He held no ambition for my sake.

—You once admired him. What did you want to be when you grew up?

His shadow. His bodyguard. His idol.

—Will he forgive you?

Always and without compunction. Crossing his hands behind his neck and leaning backward in his chair.

—You aren't asking his forgiveness but he grants it anyway. If you forgave him in his turn, what would you say?

I take back everything I've said.

telling uncle r

Uncle R is the very last relative I have in this world. He is a homely old man, a pathological liar, and he is selling the house that he and my father grew up in. He says that anything within its walls is mine. Most of the furniture is old, and in a week or two the antique dealers will arrive, bidding on tables and chairs, buying the mirrors where my grandmothers combed their hair for a hundred years. He says I should buy the house itself, but I tell him no. When I look at the tilt of the upper floors, the slant of the porch and the footsteps worn in the stone beneath the door, I feel the weight of too many lives, a century of habits not my own.

"Suit yourself," says Uncle R. "If you plan to be a jackass all your life, you might as well start right here at home."

Uncle R is seventy-two and plans to move to a senior

citizens' retreat. In the meantime he has a live-in aide and companion, a woman named Mrs. Becca, who lives alone on the second floor. She is a high-strung woman with a narrow head, and with fingers that are small and curled and pinkish, like rows of shrimp. She seems to be fond of Uncle R and periodically pulls me aside to discuss his condition.

"He talks about death a lot," she says. "I thought I should warn you. Funerals all day long, hideous stories I couldn't repeat. He seems to have a very active mind."

"I know those stories," I tell her, just to let her know who's familiar and who's not. "Shark tanks and prison camps and Indians buried alive. Did he tell you about the man who got caught in a tuna-pack machine? He came out the other end in a bunch of cans, and they had to open every one to reassemble him."

Mrs. Becca ignores me. She is peeling vegetables, leaving all the eyes in the potatoes.

"What does he say about me?" I ask. "I barely see him anymore."

"He's glad you're here." She shrugs. "He says you'll be taking a lot of things with you when you leave."

Briefly I wonder how deep her interest goes. Does she have her eye on a marble-top dresser, on the sewing machine underneath the stairs?

Uncle R's toes are on the linoleum just behind me, and I step on some of them and turn around. He is wearing a red knit bathrobe and a pair of sweatbands on his wrists. His face is thin, his blue eyes unnaturally bright.

"I didn't hear you coming," I tell him.

"That's because of my invisible slippers." Uncle R is a short man, and now seems frail in a stubborn and aggressive way. "I should be underground already, is that what you're thinking?"

"No."

"I'm going to save the both of you a lot of trouble." He leans back against the cabinets and crosses his legs. "We won't have a funeral. You'll just fold me in half and drop me into the trash. You put a ten-dollar bill in my mouth and set me out on the curb. What are you drinking?"

"Nothing yet."

"We'll fix you a scotch and water," he says, sitting down at the kitchen table. "I'll bet you barely remember this place. You were just a kid when we had holidays here. You don't understand what this house is worth."

"I know what it's worth. Anyway, I was here a year ago, last July."

"Take the table." Uncle R is back to his days as a salesman, when he peddled housewares door to door. "We had card games here that lasted nights and days. Your Uncle Karl stabbed me here, nicked me on the temple with a knife, because I beat him at this table Christmas Eve. You don't remember things like that. You were too young."

"I remember them perfectly. When everyone else was eating dinner you'd be gambling in the kitchen, snacking off the plates when we were done. Everyone said you cheated."

"I didn't need to cheat," he says. "I won by magic."

Mrs. Becca skins her finger with the peeler.

"That's what's wrong with you," he says. "You didn't stay long enough to find out who we were. You grew up alone. You don't even speak German."

"We lived all over the country," I remind him. "My

father was transferred a half dozen times. It wasn't easy to come back."

"He used to visit just enough so he wouldn't feel guilty. So he wouldn't feel bad for having deserted us. He would have stayed here if it wasn't for Winifred."

Winifred was my mother. "I don't see anything wrong with wanting to lead your own life," I tell him. "She didn't want to share a house with her husband's relatives."

"She called us drunks and degenerates!" he shouts. "We were a normal, loving family."

"What about Uncle Karl? And Uncle Edward? I heard he tried to murder his wife."

Uncle R pauses to clean his teeth with a carrot. "Uncle Edward was dead before you were born. Besides, she deserved it."

· · · · · · · ·

"This was your father's room." Uncle R insists on leading me through the house as if I have never been here. The ceilings are low and stained with waterspots and the wood floors are buckled.

"We spent years in this room together. Your father and I grew up in this room. You were supposed to be born here, right on this bed. But your mother decided to go to a hospital."

I examine a dust-mouse the size of a dog.

"The *best* thing about this room—" Uncle R's face is flushed like a young boy's "—is the closet. You can crawl through a door in the ceiling and make your way to the roof. Your father and I used to climb up there at night and watch the stars, lying there right on the edge of the roof."

"I've been through that trap door. It just leads to the attic."

He turns and stares at me. "Who's the visitor here, me or you?" But I can tell that he's pleased.

"This was Tante Lena's room." He is breathing hard from climbing the stairs but is trying not to show it. "She used to stand here by the window—right here—" he pulls me by the arm so I am standing in the very spot he's referring to "—and stay here sometimes half the night. She almost never slept. She didn't need to sleep."

"My mother never liked Tante Lena," I offer. "She thought she was too domineering."

"Your mother," says Uncle R with a yawn, "was an idiot."

. . . .

We check the attic, the seven bedrooms, and the garage. So far I have chosen a silver hand mirror, the sewing machine that might otherwise have gone to Mrs. Becca, and a small embroidered footstool with someone's initials woven all around the sides.

"Now for the basement," says Uncle R. "I've set aside some things you'll want to have." He flips on the light and we descend.

On the basement floor is an enormous heap of furniture and dishes, boxes overflowing with paper, photograph albums, clothing, books and toys. A set of porcelain floor lamps, each with life-size Oriental ladies holding up the shades, flanks the pile.

"You're out of your mind," I tell him. "I live in an apartment. I have three and a half rooms and a closet."

"Is that supposed to be my fault?" he says. "You should get a bigger place."

"I don't want these things, Uncle R."

"It's not a matter of wanting them or not. They can't be sold. You don't have a choice."

I look at the stacks of furniture and clothes, including two fur coats and a row of foxes biting each other's tails. Some of the things are beautiful, in fact, but they aren't mine. The massive dressers have claws for feet and the armchairs have wings: this is the opposite of my life, a heavy, well-endowed existence built on certainty, determination, drive. My own life is reflected more by cotton and rattan.

"Look at this." Uncle R holds up a photograph. It's a sepia-colored woman in a floor-length dress. She stares at the camera intensely, as if rehearsing for the moment when I'll reach down and dust her off.

"You have her nose," he says. "A bump in the middle and a little ball on the end. Very unusual. Actually there's quite a likeness."

I hand it back to him and sit down in a velvet chair.

"It's Tante Lena as a young woman," he says. "Nearly six feet tall by the age of fourteen. She could put out a fire with her hands."

"I'll take the picture, Uncle R, if you'll leave me alone about the rest."

"This was hers," he says, patting a roll-top. "This was your Tante Lena's desk."

"I'm going upstairs to take a bath. I'll take the picture if you want."

"You'll take all of it. Every scrap."

I reach the steps and turn around. Uncle R is facing his possessions, gathered there as if waiting for a speech. He spreads out his hands in astonishment. "Do you believe this woman?" he says.

. . . .

To pass the time we play pinochle. Mrs. Becca has never played but we need a third, so she sits perched on the edge of her seat, tallying points.

"What do you say we raise the stakes?" says Uncle R. "Give the game a little spice."

"What do you mean? A dollar?"

"I had more than that in mind." He tightens the belt of his bathrobe, cracks his wrists. "Let's say we wager my grandmother's desk. You don't have a desk like that at home. Win the round and we take it from the pile; I'll even chop it into firewood myself."

"What if I lose? Why don't we bet that you go to a doctor. He might be able to tell you what you've got."

"My health is fine." He crosses his legs. "Nothing that a few pleasant years below a garden can't take care of. I'll take out the lamps. Double or nothing keeps the lot."

"You don't look well, Uncle R."

"Oh, is that your opinion?" He raps my cards with a knuckle. "You should worry about your own life for a change. You live like a hermit. A single window the size of a dime and some naked walls. There's something strange about a person who wants to live in a place like that. It's not fit for a mole."

"Suit yourself." I trump his king with the nine of hearts.

He pauses, then spreads his cards like a fan. "We never used doctors when I was growing up. Not unless we had to get rid of someone in a hurry. Then we called up for a quick injection, the way they kill criminals. That's what happened to your great Aunt Emma. She was fine, perfectly healthy. But everyone said she was just taking up space."

"I'll take the picture and the things I found upstairs. But that's the end."

"She was a witch. A real pain in the ass. I'm not asking you to take it all at once. You start with a chair. A miniature couch for your apartment."

"I don't need a chair."

"Or a doll-sized rug. Maybe a goddamn silver thimble you can use as a bathtub!"

Mrs. Becca jumps up and spills her coffee on the cards. The liquid rolls across the face of a king of spades; then it follows a cleft in the table, seeping quickly toward the edge.

"Great," says Uncle R. "Magnificent." He mops the coffee with the belt of his bathrobe, wringing it out above his cup. "I always knew one day I'd be sitting at a table, just like this, across from a woman with a scorepad in her hand. We'd be sitting around like regular people, except that one of us was nuts and one was a hermit. The nut would have coffee stains on his clothes and the hermit would sit there like a stone, and even if he offered her a couple souvenirs from one of the nicest houses in the state of New York, a goddamn landmark, she'd sit there like a deaf-mute and refuse to answer."

"I can't take the furniture, Uncle R."

He dries the belt against his leg. "You'll come around. I can feel it."

* * * * * * * *

After dinner he tells us a story. Mrs. Becca has dished out ice cream with frozen peaches and is pretending to wash the pots. Bits of rice still cling to the dishes in the drainer.

"We were on our way to a wedding," he says, "your father and your Uncle Edward and I, and your great-grandmother at the wheel. And right smack in front of our car is the Henderson kid, sitting in the middle of the road by the tracks. We hear the train coming and figure he's waiting for freight cars. He used to throw stones at the guys on top, hoping they'd get mad enough to throw down coal in return. Sometimes he'd get enough to heat the house for a week. So we honk at him, tell him to beat it. But the kid stands up—" here Uncle R would usually stand, but now just straightens in his chair "—looks us straight in the eye and walks out onto the tracks. Just stands there with his eyes wide open until it comes up and kills him."

"This is another decapitation story, isn't it?" Uncle R has a number of versions, each one ending with a headless man in the trunk of a car. "Can you hold off on that until I've finished my dinner?"

Uncle R begins cutting his ice cream with a knife and fork. "Weak stomach?" he rasps. "We had to piece him back together right here in the kitchen—right here on the maple table like it was an undertaker's slab! We didn't have time for weak stomachs. We didn't have that *luxury!*"

I can see his next sentence taking shape, his accusations dropping into place. I have had it too easy, my entire childhood I was entertained, I have no idea what hardship means and am therefore yellow, flabby, pale and unformed. But Uncle R seems suddenly tired. He puts his head down on the table, the wisps of white hair on his freckled scalp drifting into the ice cream. "When was it that your father died?" he asks. "Before or after your great Aunt Emma?"

"After," I tell him.

"Sometimes I miss your father like hell. He was my younger brother."

"I know that."

"And when was it that he died? I think I forgot."

"In sixty-nine. October third. You remember that, Uncle R. You went to the funeral."

"And who read the eulogy?"

I have to think back. It's hard to think with Uncle R's head on the table in front of me. "You did."

"And what did I say?"

"You said my father was the finest man you ever knew. You said he was a family man, that he loved his family more than anything else."

He lifts his head off the table. "That's what I thought."

. . . .

The picture of Tante Lena finds its way into my room. It's on the nightstand, and watches me when I sleep. Such symbols aren't lost on Uncle R. Under his direction I head for the basement once again, selecting additional items to take home. These are a maple rocking chair, a small oriental rug in red and gray, and the ring of foxes biting each other's tails.

This last choice amuses Uncle R. "I guess those look good with a sweatshirt," he says. It's true I won't wear the foxes, and the idea of animals stuffed or skinned has always seemed to me fairly repulsive, but there's something whimsical in the hinged and furry mouths that I can picture on a wall. Every hour or two we journey to the basement, for lack of anything better to do.

"We're just going to look," he says. "To browse. There's one other thing that you haven't seen." Soon, though, he's insisting that I have to take the object home. "You owe me this," he says. "You wouldn't have been born if it weren't for me. I must have saved your father's life a dozen times."

"Not the last time, though," I say.

He picks up a vase but I shake my head.

"You're deranged. They were right. Tante Lena and Uncle Karl. They always said it was disappointing the way you turned out."

"That's ridiculous. Uncle Karl was nearly blind when I was born, and Tante Lena must have been ninety. They didn't know me. Both of them died when I was small."

"So he was blind," says Uncle R. "He had ears that you wouldn't believe. He heard even better in the dark. And Tante Lena, she was the strongest woman alive. One day it was raining, just like this, but the gutters were jammed full with leaves and the roof was starting to leak. So Tante Lena climbed up the drainpipe herself, shinnied up the side of the house in the pouring rain to dig out those leaves. Your father and I were sitting here playing checkers, on this very board, and we saw her pass by the window on her way to the roof. Like a rabbit," he says. "You can still see the marks from her boot-toes on the wall."

"Uncle R—"

"I wouldn't expect you to be interested," he snaps. "You always hated your own great-grandmother."

"I wasn't old enough to hate her."

"Chocolate-covered raisins," he says. "She used to feed them to you from the palm of her hand."

"Those are stories, Uncle R."

"Well of course they're stories. What else is left?" He puts down the vase and weighs an ashtray in his hand. "What a joke," he says. "That you're the only one left. Out of such a family we should all boil down to you. Do you think you can stay another week?"

"I have things to take care of. I left the cats with a neighbor."

"Cats," says Uncle R. "Nothing to go home to but a house full of cat hair."

"I have other things to go home for."

"Such as?" He turns to face me and I have to concentrate to bring the twelve white walls of my apartment into view. It's true that except for the cats I have cleared out a lot. The more I throw away the better I feel. But this is something Uncle R would not understand. "Organization," I say at last. "Cleanliness."

"I'm overwhelmed," says Uncle R.

. . . .

He tells stories, one after the next, and wonders why I don't repay them with my own. What could be worthwhile telling Uncle R? When I try to tell him about my job, or about the families in the building where I live, the telling seems pointless to us both.

"Who was the kid? What did he have to do with the lady in green?" Uncle R squints at my narration, impatient with people he doesn't know. "It's in the delivery," he says. "It's like a joke. You learn to build up to the climax, take

your audience along. Mostly you have to start with something good."

I could tell him that this is what I love about him most:
the authority with which he tells a lie. Instead I ask him
for the story of the rosebush.

"You could tell that one," he says. "I'm sure you know it
well enough."

"I'll get to the middle and forget."

"Liar," he says. "You could tell that story in your sleep."
He cleans his fingernails with a tweezers. "Just give me
the beginning. Start me off and I'll take over."

"I wasn't there. I wasn't born."

"What year was it?" he insists.

"Twenty-two."

"Twenty-four. You're doing fine. And who bought the
rosebush?"

"Her husband bought it. Tante Lena's husband."

"Very good. And what happened when he brought the
rosebush home?"

I try to imagine the house as it must have been. I have
heard this story twenty times. It's meant to illustrate our
crustiness, the family's unwavering hostile stance in the
face of kindness, persistent sympathy, love.

"They'd been arguing all day, they were out of money.
Her husband took the last of his paycheck from her purse
and bought a rosebush, just to make up for the things
they'd said. He was a gardener and he had a way with
plants. Tante Lena thought he'd gone to pay the rent, but
he came back with a rosebush and some dirt. She was
furious when she saw him coming up the walk."

"What did the rosebush look like?" Uncle R sinks back
in a chair and shuts his eyes.

"It was yellow, nearly in bloom. Even my father said it

was the most beautiful rosebush he'd ever seen: tiny yellow buds in such profusion it was impossible to count them. He was just a boy at the time but he always said he remembered it perfectly, my great-grandfather trailing up the walk with a rosebush in a yellow bucket."

"Your great-grandfather. What was he like?"

"What was he like?" Uncle R's robe has fallen open to reveal a pale white thigh, slender and almost hairless.

I close my eyes. "His name is Anthony. He's very handsome, with a huge mustache and a red bandanna at his neck. He likes to tell jokes."

"What happens next?"

"He takes the rosebush up the steps of the porch, but Tante Lena sees him coming. She grabs the rosebush out of his hands, straight up out of the dirt so the thorns are cutting deep into her palms. She doesn't feel it, she's got arms like a stevedore and she throws the roses into the street, throws them up over the gate and into the gutter."

"Then what?"

"He left and didn't come back. She planted the roses by the side of the house and they bloomed here for years." We sit with the story between us now. "Is that what you wanted, Uncle R? I still don't feel I have it right. Did I get it right?"

Uncle R sits up and looks at his watch. "When I'm dead," he says. "That's when you'll learn to get it right."

. . . .

In the middle of the night my uncle falls on his way to the bathroom. When I help him back to bed he refuses to look at me, and in desperation I ask him for a story.

"I don't know any stories," he says, his face turned toward the wall.

"A story about my father. Or about Tante Lena."

He is still facing the wall. "Those are old stories," he says. "I don't remember the endings."

In the morning I lift the car keys from the nail. The car is a massive old machine, brown and rounded at the corners, with a huge steel smile between the headlights. In the overstuffed driver's seat I put the key in the ignition, knowing that this is the car that drove us to my father's funeral, and to great Aunt Emma's, and even earlier to Tante Lena's. I can almost picture the old lady in the back seat behind me. I see her deep blue eyes in the rear view mirror, the high black collar of her dress. She nods at me and I see her nose somewhat like mine. I begin to believe that Tante Lena could do anything she wanted. She could climb a waterspout like a spider in the rain, or glide past the window on her way to the moon.

It is almost two hours later that I pull into a garden shop. Although they don't have any yellow ones I find a large, sturdy, white-budded rosebush that might look yellow in the sun. I imagine the look on Uncle R's face when he sees it, and I am surprised at how excited I feel, at how completely satisfied the purchase has made me. As I pull into the drive I see the sun shining on the face of the house, lighting it, and Mrs. Becca standing on the edge of the porch. She catches sight of me and steps down onto the lawn. She is running toward me now across the bright green grass, her handkerchief over her face, and for the first time in my life I feel everything falling into place, the past taking shape all around me.